PRASES for *Teachin*

Review #1: Review by Wilma - *Goodreads*

Review Rating: 5 Stars

"This first effort by the author is a real page-turner! I wanted to keep reading to find out what in the world would happen next to the goodhearted protagonist, who kept inadvertently getting in trouble. Lots of philosophical gems strewn throughout; good descriptions; great storytelling! Well worth reading."

Review #2: Review by Arya Fomonyuy - *Readers' Favorite*

Review Rating: 5 Stars

"*Teachings of a Shaman: A Story of Deliverance & Redemption* by Corey Stultz is a gripping, inspiring story that… is so beautifully told, readers will find themselves following the protagonist and caring so much about him. It's a spiritual adventure fraught with lessons about life, inner freedom, and love. I enjoyed the great writing, the strong plot with its surprising turns, the insights, and the emotional depth of the story. Corey Stultz has written a story that will bring light and love into the hearts of readers. *Teachings of a Shaman: A Story of Deliverance & Redemption* is a gem and a wonderful piece of entertainment for readers. It was a straight read for me."

TEACHINGS of a SHAMAN

A Story of Deliverance & Redemption

Corey Stultz

"A gripping, inspiring story... a gem and a wonderful piece of entertainment!"
— Arya Fomonyuy, *Readers Favorite*

TEACHINGS
of a
SHAMAN

COREY STULTZ

Cover designed by Illumination Graphics, Inc.

Website—coreystultz.com—designed by College Web Pro

TV/film/other media rights inquiries—corey@coreystultz.com

coreystultz.com

Teachings of a Shaman is sold worldwide, exclusively on Amazon.
Published by Halcyon Press.

ISBN-13: 978-0-692-88615-1
ISBN-10: 0-692-88615-X
LCCN: 2017907041

To my children, Sidney and Jeremy:

I love you with all my heart.

I will always be there for you.

I promise.

1

Rubbing the sleep from his eyes, Dwayne pushed himself up to a seated position and looked around. Holes and graffiti riddled the walls, and bare wires protruded from the ceiling. A few feet away, his friend lay sleeping on a throw rug. "Hey, Mitch," he said, nudging him with his foot. "Wake up."

But Mitch didn't move.

"Come on. We have to go to work."

Still, there was no movement.

"Dammit, Mitch! I said we—" He yanked off his friend's blanket. But the man he just uncovered wasn't Mitch. Nor was he alive.

From where he sat, Dwayne scanned the interior of the abandoned rowhome once more. "Mitch! Are you in here or not?"

"Yeah," his buddy moaned, scratching himself as he emerged from around the corner. "What time is it?"

"I don't know." He looked out the broken window. "Daytime."

"Smart-ass. Who's your friend?"

"Beats me."

"What'd he do? Overdose?"

"I guess so."

"He must have scored some good shit. Did you check to see if he has any left?"

"No."

"Well, look! Flip him over. Where's his rig?"

"It's right here." Dwayne inspected the syringe that was still hanging from the individual's vein. "Nope, he shot it all."

"Fuck! Check his pockets."

Brimming with hope, he shoved his hand down the man's pants and felt around. "Nope."

"Dammit! C'mon, let's go."

Darting outside, they jumped in Dwayne's car and sped away.

As they neared the first intersection, Mitch looked in the rearview mirror. His eyes widened. "I think something's wrong with your car."

"A lot's wrong with my car," Dwayne replied, keeping his face taut as he continued to shave on the way to their destination. "Why?"

"Because we're leaving a vapor trail like a jet, except ours isn't white; it's black."

"Yeah, I know. My girlfriend's dad is a mechanic. He says I need a tune up, an alternator, and a whole bunch of stuff."

"I guess that would explain the clicking noises I heard when I was trying to start it, huh?"

"Yeah."

"How did you two meet, anyway?"

"Who?"

"You and your girl. What's her name again? Jasmine?"

"No. 'Jackie.' She works at the pretzel place in the mall. I'd always see her when I went there. Eventually, I started buying pretzels just to have an excuse to talk to her."

"Oh. And then you asked her out?"

"No. She asked me out."

"What? She asked *you* out? Why didn't you ask *her* out?"!

"I couldn't get up the nerve. Every time I tried, my heart started racing so bad, I couldn't even breathe."

"Then how'd she know you liked her?"

"Because one day I decided I was going to ask her out no matter what happened, and I wasn't going to leave the mall until I did. But every time I made it up to the counter, I chickened out and ended up just buying a pretzel from her."

"So?"

"So after I bought about seven pretzels in three hours, she pretty much figured it out. Lucky for me, her car was broke down, so she asked me if I could drive her home when she got off work."

Mitch burst out laughing. "Boy, are you stupid!"

"Why am I stupid?"

"Didn't you say her dad's a mechanic?"

"Yeah."

"Well, do you think a mechanic is ever going to let his daughter's car break down? I guarantee whatever she drives was fine."

"Hey, yeah!" Dwayne hollered from inside the shirt he was changing out of. "I bet she just made that up and used it as an excuse for the two of us to hang out together."

"Woah, nobody can get anything by you, can they, dude?" Mitch laughed as he pulled into the parking lot of a home improvement store. "Okay, we're here. Are you ready?"

"I don't know." Dwayne smirked. "You tell me. Do I look ready?"

Peering over at him, Mitch gazed at his accomplice's shiny black shoes, dress pants, and slicked back hairdo. "Yeah, I'd say you look ready."

Dwayne gave him a wink, exited the vehicle, and poked his head back in the window. "And what's the number two rule of shoplifting?" he asked.

Mitch grinned. "Enter the store, looking like you own it."

"That's right. Now sit tight, and pop the trunk as soon as you see me come back out."

"Gotcha!"

Dwayne strolled up to the entrance, grabbed a cart, and made his way to the rear of the store.

As he approached the hardware department, he noticed two people standing in the entryway. One was a manager, the other a vendor. "Excuse me," he said. "Can I squeeze by you, please?"

"Certainly, sir," the manager replied, moving out of his way. "Can I help you with something?"

"Yes. Where would I find power tools?"

"Right over there." He gestured. "You can't miss 'em."

"Thank you."

In no time, Dwayne located a power drill, a nail gun, and a chainsaw. Without hesitation, he placed all three items in his cart and headed back up front. Before exiting the final aisle and coming into view, he paused to observe the nearby employees. All of them were busy. "Here goes nothing," he mumbled, pushing his cart between two unattended registers and out the store.

Seeing that he was on his way, Mitch pressed the trunk release button and started the engine.

Dwayne loaded the car and hopped back in the passenger seat. "Okay, let's get out of here!"

Within minutes, they arrived at their next stop: the pawn shop.

No sooner had Mitch parked the car than he was unloading it. "Thunk!" He accidentally banged one of the boxes into the trunk lid.

Dwayne shot him a dirty look. "Be careful!"

"Yeah, I hear ya. Just grab the last box and come on."

Inside, a woman wearing a pleasant smile greeted them. "Good afternoon, gentlemen. May I help you?"

"Yes, uh—" Dwayne glanced at her nametag. "Bertha. Hi. We have some tools we'd like to sell."

"Okay," she replied, entering the chainsaw's specifications into her computer. Then she leaned down to her screen and studied the results. "Now, let's see what we—" Bertha's smile suddenly disappeared, her piercing eyes falling upon them. Then, without saying a word, she just turned around and walked away.

About a minute later, she returned with Ruby, the owner.

Chewing on the nub of a cigar, the obese man waddled over to her computer, scrutinizing Dwayne and Mitch along the way.

Squinting one eye, Dwayne attempted to reciprocate the pretentious man's intimidating once-over as he trudged by.

Ruby grabbed the closest stool and lowered himself upon it. "Pah-shhh!" The inanimate cushion hissed in agony as it absorbed every ounce of his weight, collapsing to the thickness of a pancake.

"See?" Bertha pointed to the screen. "Right there."

Ruby looked at the information. Then he removed the clump of tobacco from the corner of his mouth and glared at the two youths. "What are you two numskulls trying to pull?"

Dwayne tried to look innocent. "What do you mean, sir?"

"Don't you play dumb with me; this shit's so hot, it might as well be on fire! I wasn't born yesterday, boys."

"What! Now how the fuck do you—" Mitch managed to blurt out before Dwayne elbowed him. "Oww!"

"What my friend here was attempting to say was, 'much of what your type of establishment acquires for resale is often originally obtained via illegitimate means, sir. Therefore, hypothetically speaking, if that were to be the circumstance with these three fine products, why would you refuse our proposition to engage in what would surely result in a mutually beneficial transaction this afternoon?'"

Ruby gawked at Dwayne in complete silence. Then he turned to Mitch. "What in the *hell* did he just say? Illegittah— Hypothettah— Is he foreign?"! Ruby's eyes darted back to Dwayne. "Are you foreign?"! He yelled in Dwayne's face. "You people need to stay in your own dadgum country until you can talk good English like us, before you go coming over here, acting like you own everything!"

Mitch blinked a few times, his brow furrowing in confusion. "No, he ain't foreign! His smartness and big words just sorta spill out of his mouth so fast that you can't understand him sometimes!"

"Oh. So what's his problem then?"

"He wants to know why you don't want to buy the shit we stole!"

"Because it's too new."

"Too new? How the hell can something be too new?"!

"By looking up the model and serial numbers on this here internet thing. This chainsaw ain't even been on the market but for a couple *months*! The stuff you boys boost has to have been in the stores for at least a year or more, so I look like I'm running a legit business. Now get this shit out of here before it burns a hole in my counter. Go on, now! Scoot, scoot, scoot!" He swooshed them away as if they were little kids.

Outside, Mitch helped Dwayne reload the car. "Now what?" he grumbled.

"Now we have to go to Plan B, that's all."

"Plan B?"

"Yup. Rule number four: Always have a backup plan."

"Okay. So what's Plan B?"

"Head down to Howard Avenue."

"Howard Avenue? What's on— Oh, that's right! Jed! Yeah, he'll take it!"

"I know. I was just hoping we wouldn't have to drive the extra fifteen miles out of the way, though."

"Eh, look at it this way. If you didn't know the guy, we wouldn't have to go the extra distance, but that would also mean we wouldn't have any money for today."

"—and we'd be sick as shit in a couple hours." Dwayne bowed his head. "Okay, you're right. Let's go."

Arriving at Jed's Pawn Shop, Dwayne hustled to the door, yanked it open, and whistled.

The lanky old man inside looked up.

Dwayne held his finger up, and rotated it by his ear.

Jed cracked a smile, winked at him, and obtained the attention of his assistant – all without missing a beat. "Take your time deciding between the two necklaces, Mrs. Cavanaugh," he said, putting the more expensive one around her neck. "But I think *this* one really makes your eyes sparkle. By the way, this is Nancy.

She's my jewelry expert here in the shop. I'm going to ask that she take over for me, as I need to tend to something in the back."

"Oh, sure, Jed, honey," the old lady replied, opening her eyes extra wide, looking at herself in the mirror. "I remember Nancy from the last time I was here."

Jed weaved his way through his jumbled backroom, to the rear entrance of his store. "Howdy, fellas!" he hollered, jerking the door open. "Whatcha got for me today?"

"Power tools, Jed!" Dwayne replied. "Nice ones too."

"Excellent. Can you carry them over here for me?" he asked, hobbling over to his workstation, clutching his lower back. "This damn dampness really draws in my joints. Have y'all heard when the rain's supposed to move on outta here?"

Mitch's face contorted. "Pssst! Hey, Dwayne! What's that old coot talking about? It ain't raining outside; it's sunny."

"Shhh! Just agree with him. As long as he pays us, who cares. If he says 'it's raining,' it's raining."

"What'd you say?" Jed asked, sitting down at his desk. "I couldn't hear ya."

"This evening," Dwayne replied, setting the merchandise next to him. "The rain's supposed to move out of here this evening."

"Good." He leaned forward and examined everything. Then he buried his face in his laptop and pecked away at its keyboard. "Oh, yes. Very nice." He viewed the results of his research. "And just what did the two of you want for all three?"

"Well, the goin' rate around town is 40% of retail." Mitch opened negotiations.

"Oh no it ain't, ya boob!" Jed whirled around to confront his antagonist. "I heard it's more like 18%!"

"Eighteen?"! Mitch's nostrils flared. "Now you listen here, you son of a—"

"Halt!" Dwayne raised his hands. "Stop right there! I don't know why you two can't ever get along, but we don't have time for your little pissing contest today. Look, let's save forty minutes of fighting and agree to the usual 33% you always give us. Right now, Pops. Decide. Yay or nay?"

"Aww-gee-whiz, boy!" Jed complained. "Now you went and took all the fun outta flusterin' ol' Prissy Pants. But yeah, you got yourself a deal. Hold on. Lemme calculate this real quick."

"Prissy Pants?"! Mitch exclaimed. "Did that old fart just call me Prissy Pants?"!

"Yeah, now shut up."

"But why—"

"Mitch! Shut up!"

"Let's see, we got four hundred, four fifty, and five fifty... add it all up... and then multiply by point-three-three..." Jed articulated his thought process aloud as he poked numbers on his old-time adding machine. "That means I owe you an even $400. How would you like it? Do you want me to give each of you three crisp, new, $50 bills?" He smiled.

Mitch's eyes lit up. "Yeah, buddy! That sounds gr—"

"Stop right there!" Dwayne said. "Jed, you're allowed to get your kicks by messing with Mitch if that tickles your pickle, but you are *not* permitted to screw around with my money. You got that, old man?"

"Huh? Oh, you each get *four* fifties, don't ya? Sorry about— Hey! Stop! What the hell are you doing?"! Jed watched in horror as Dwayne pointed a forty-four caliber handgun at his laptop.

"I told you not to fuck around with my money, Pops. Now… you have an insanely short amount of time to locate your mathematical error and recalculate."

"Okay! Okay! I found it!" Jed attempted to convince him. "400, 450, and 550 total 1,400, not 1,200! It was an honest mistake, I swear!"

"And what's 33% of $1,400?"

"$462!" The elderly man rectified his so-called honest mistake, his fingers trembling. "Seriously, it's $462!"

"There you go. That's better. But you forgot to add in the penalty fee."

"Penalty fee? What penalty fee?"

"There's a tiny $38 penalty fee for trying to dupe us. That brings the total to an even $500. So you can feel free to give each of us *five* $50 bills, not three like you originally said."

"Penalty fee, my ass! I told you it was an honest—"

"Click." Dwayne pulled the hammer back with his thumb and shut one eye, threatening to pull the trigger.

"Alright! Alright! $250 each!"

"It's a pleasure doing business with you, Jed. Next time though, make sure you properly calculate what you owe us, okay?"

"Yes, sir."

"Very well, then." Dwayne looked over at Mitch. "Come on, Prissy Pants. Let's go."

"I'm com— Hey, dickhead! Don't call me that!"

Mitch followed Dwayne outside, put on his sunglasses, and prepared to leave. But before they had a chance to drive off, Jed appeared in the doorway. "Hey! Wait a minute!" He flailed his arms. "Come back!"

Mitch stepped on the brake. "Now what's he want?" he asked, removing his sunglasses.

"Beats me. Just sit tight a minute, and I'll go see." Dwayne walked back to meet him returned.

"Well?" Mitch said. "What was all that about?"

"Jed wanted us to have this." Dwayne handed him an umbrella. "He said we're supposed to use it until the rain tapers off."

2

A short time later, Dwayne had an idea. "Hey, stop driving for a minute."

Mitch glanced in the rearview mirror. "Dude, I can't just stop in the middle of the road. There's like six thousand cars behind us."

"Well, pull into one of these businesses or something." He gestured out his window.

Mitch turned into the parking lot of a fast food restaurant.

"Before we head back, I want to call one of my connections who's just a few more miles south of here. His shit's always good, and it's typically a little cheaper. And if he'll give us five for four, we can split the cost, share the last gram, and still have a hundred bucks left over. Sound cool?"

"Yeah, go for it."

Dwayne placed the call.

"Hello," his friend answered.

"Yo, Stick! It's Dwayne."

"Dwayne!" Stick shouted over the jukebox blaring in the background. "What's going on?"

"Not much. Hey, listen. I'm down in your neck of the woods, and I was wondering if you could help me out."

"Yeah, probably. What are you looking for? Boy or girl?"

"Boy."

"How much?"

"Five."

"Yeah, I can do that."

"Cool! Where are you? Can I meet you right now?"

"Sure. I'm at the Hidden Treasure. Come by whenever you want. I'll even let you buy me a beer when you get here." He laughed.

"The Hidden Treasure? What made you go there?"

"Eh, sometimes a man has to treat himself to the finer things in life, you know what I mean?"

"Yeah. Okay, we'll be there in about twenty minutes."

"Sounds good. I'll see ya soon."

Dwayne shoved his phone back into his pocket. "Alright, pull back out onto the road and make a left."

Mitch looked at him. "Go back the way we came from?"

"Yeah."

"Okay, you're the boss," he said, turning the key. "But what's the Hidden Treasure?"

"Oh, you've never been there before?"

"If I had, I wouldn't be asking, now, would I?"

"It's a swanky strip club."

"What's 'swanky' mean? Sleazy?"

"No. The opposite. Fancy and high-class."

"That's cool."

"Yeah, it'll be fun," Dwayne said, noticing Mitch's attire. "Hey, there's a place up here between the church and the Burger Bonanza; it has a sign out front that says 'Heaven's Helpers.' Pull in there."

"Why?"

"Just do it!"

"Okay, okay!" Mitch pulled into the driveway. "Now what?"

"Look, the place we're going to has a dress code, and they're not going to let you in, looking like you do. Inside that building in front of you are volunteers who help the needy. Go in there, tell them you're poor, and—"

"But I really *am* poor."

"I know. Just listen. Tell them you're poor, and that you need a set of nice clothes—shoes and everything. Be respectful, don't curse, show gratitude, and take no more than what you absolutely need. Do you hear me?"

"Yeah. But why all the rules and niceness all of a sudden?"

"I got my reasons. Now go get some clothes and meet me back here in ten minutes. I have something I need to do. And don't dillydally because I still have to make another stop after we meet Stick… and then I have to hit my house. And I have plans at seven!"

"Okay, Mr. Important, I'm on my— Wait! Did you say you're going to stop off at *your* house? You mean, your parents' place?"!

"Yeah. There's something that I need to get from there, and I also have to shower, so I really don't have a choice."

"You're fucking insane! Come on, man, don't take a chance on going back there!"

"'I *have* to,' I said! And what did I tell you about cursing! Now, no more dropping of the f-bomb while we're in the church's parking lot, you got that?"!

"Why not?"

"Just don't! Now go!" Dwayne said, walking away in the opposite direction.

Shrugging off his companion's peculiar demeanor, Mitch strolled up to the outbuilding and entered. He was instantly spellbound, for the interior of the structure was warmly illuminated by nothing but candles and Christmas lights, the hardwood floor shined brilliantly from being routinely polished, and the rustic wall paneling brought back fond childhood memories of when he used to hang out in his grandparents' basement with his Pap Pap.

To his left, an antique wooden radio was playing the most beautiful choir music he'd ever heard. To his right, three elderly women were sitting in rocking chairs, crocheting. And in the middle stood Mitch, gawking at the all the lights reflecting off the wall-mounted crucifixes as if he'd been hypnotized.

Just then, the lady sitting in the middle pushed her glasses higher on the bridge of her nose and smiled. "May I help you, child?" she asked in a soft voice.

Mitch didn't say anything at first. For he was once again captivated by the Christmas lights, except this time, they were bouncing around in the woman's spectacles. The incredible sight bestowed upon him an unprecedented state of relaxation. "You look like Mrs. Claus," he said, his eyelids falling half closed.

"Excuse me?" Helen tilted her head.

"You know. Santa's wife. And I feel like I'm in some kind of magical toy shop or something." Mitch continued to survey his surroundings. "Yup. Like in his clothing department." He nodded.

"I see." Helen tried to suppress her giggling.

Then Mitch noticed the yarn leading up to her lap. "What are you making?"

"We're crocheting afghans to enter in this fall's county fair. After they're judged, they'll be auctioned off, and the proceeds will go to those who are less fortunate."

"That's nice." Mitch scratched around in his hair, still taking in his surroundings.

Noting the condition of his clothing, the woman on the end put her crochet down and looked directly at Mitch. "I sure am glad you stopped in here just now."

"You are? Why's that?"

"Because I'm tired of sitting in that ol' chair." She stood up and stretched. "I need something to do. How about I pick out a few things for you? I bet I could find some stuff to make you look real snazzy."

"Aw, that'd be great!"

"Excellent. What size is your waist?"

"I don't know. I think I'm a 30. Maybe a 28."

"Heavens-to-Betsy, you're a skinny-minny! We have to put some meat on your bones. What have you had to eat so far today?"

"Nothing."

"Land 'o Mercy, we can't have that!" She grabbed what appeared to be a sandwich out of the Burger Bonanza bag that was sitting on the table and handed it to him.

"That's very kind of you, but I can't eat your dinner."

"Oh, that's not my dinner. We, uh... we have certain days that we offer special deals and contests, and it just so happens that you're today's winner!" She leaned in close to him and lowered her voice. "Now tell me, sonny, do you like onions?"

"Yeah. Why?"

"Because this thing's *loaded* with 'em." She winked at him. "Now you park yourself next to Mable and get to eating your Bonus Burger Prize, and I'll pick you out a real nice pair of dress pants. Oh! And what size shoes do you wear?"

"Ten," Mitch replied, unwrapping what turned out to be a whopping, one-third pound hamburger. "Woah!" He salivated over all the gooey cheese and sautéed onions squishing out from under the fresh potato roll.

Peeping over the top of some furniture, Henrietta took a moment to observe him enjoying it. Figuring he had no idea what his neck circumference or sleeve length was, she eyed his stature and gave it her best guess in selecting a shirt for him.

Then she stood in the center of the room, making odd clicking noises with her mouth as she looked around. "Let's see..." she murmured. "What else can I—" Suddenly, her eyes lit up, and she dashed over to a bin by the radio.

Bending over at the waist, she hollered, "Ah-ha!" from deep inside the 36-inch-tall box.

"Stand up, Henrietta!" Helen laughed. "You look ridiculous!"

"Got 'em!" She popped up to an erect stance.

"Got what?"

"Hair gel, cologne, and a hair brush."

Helen smiled. "Hey, Mable," she whispered. "How do you like the new 'Burger-Bonus-Prize' thing that we're apparently doing now?"

"Pffft! Yeah, I know." She chortled. "I'll go get her another hamburger from next door a little later."

By the time Mitch finished eating his "prize," Henrietta had picked out a whole new outfit for him. "Here you go." She smiled.

"Oh my, how do I ever thank you?"

"How? That's easy! By marching right over there and trying on all this stuff for me, to make sure it fits."

"What? But I was just—"

"Go on, now! Right over there." She pointed to the dressing room. "I can hardly wait to see how it all looks on you."

A short time later, Mitch emerged from the fitting room, wearing his new clothes.

Henrietta spied him right away. "Hey-hey, look at you!" She clasped her hands together and smiled. "Go to the mirror and take a gander at yourself. What do you think?"

Mitch walked over and stood in front of the full-length mirror. "Is that really me?" he gasped, turning around to check out his backside.

"My gracious, you *are* snazzy!" Mable said.

"Spiffy!" Helen added. "Yes, *very* spiffy! What a fine, handsome young man you are."

Mitch couldn't stop grinning.

"And now, for the finishing touch!" Henrietta said, smashing a glob of hair gel atop his head when he wasn't looking.

"Whoa!" Mitch jumped.

"Settle down, youngin'! I'm not through with you yet! Now stiffen up your neck like this," she said, jutting her jaw outward, revealing her bottom row of teeth.

Mitch mimicked her.

"Helen!" Mable smacked her arm. "Look quick! You're missing it!"

Helen peered over at Henrietta and Mitch. "Oh, my heavens!" She burst out laughing. "The pair of them look like a couple of lizards fighting over a fly!"

When they finished gussying him up, he waved goodbye and made his way to the exit. He reached for the doorknob – but he didn't turn it. Instead, he surprisingly turned around and walked back to Henrietta.

"Is something wrong, dear?" she asked

"No—" his voice cracked. "It's just that nobody's ever—" Mitch cleared his throat and wiped his eye. "I just wanted to say, 'thank you,' that's all." He leaned in and kissed her cheek.

Once he left, the three ladies simply sat back down, smiled at one another, and returned to their crocheting.

Outside, Mitch jogged over the car, opened the door, and jumped in.

"What took you so long?"! Dwayne asked, looking over at him. "Mitch! Is that really you? Look at your clothes! And your hair!"

"Ha-ha! Yeah, I'm *snazzy*!"

"Snazzy?"

"Yup! Spiffy, too! The Heaven's Helpers people said so."

"They said you look— Hey, why do you smell like onions?"

"Because I won the bonus prize."

"What are you talking about? What bonus prize?"

"Today was Bonus Bonanza Biggie Burger Day, or something like that. Whatever it was, it was darn delicious! Boy, you missed out! What were you doing, anyways?"

"I walked over to the church next door."

Mitch became still. He looked at Dwayne. "You go inside?"

"Yeah. It's been a while since I've been to church, so I went inside and... you know."

"No. I don't. What did you do?"

"I, uh... hung out with God for a little while. Just me and Him," Dwayne replied, looking downward.

"I didn't know you and God were tight like that. Good for you, dude."

"Really?" He raised his head.

"Yeah."

A moment of silence ensued. "All right," Dwayne said, before things became awkward, "start this baby up! We have places to go!"

Mitch turned the key. "Click-click-click-click-click." The car refused to start. "Uh-oh."

"Try it again."

"Click-click-click-click-click."

"Motherrrr-darn it!"

"Wait! There's Henrietta!" Mitch pointed to her. "She's coming out of the building."

"There's who?"

"Henrietta! The nice angel-lady person." Mitch stuck his head out the window. "Hey, Henrietta! Our car won't start. Can you fix it for us? You know, bless it or something?"

"I can't bless your car, honey!" She laughed.

"Just try."

Giggling, the elderly woman outstretched her hands toward Dwayne's jalopy and wiggled her fingers. "Beedle-biddle, beedle-biddle!"

Mitch lowered his butt back into his seat and turned the key. "Vah'roooom!" The vehicle fired up.

Henrietta stopped laughing, and her face losing all expression.

"Thank you!" Mitch yelled, backing out of his parking spot.

The bewildered lady looked down at her fingers and wriggled them once more. "Beedle-biddle, beedle-biddle?" she whispered.

3

This is going to be awesome!" Mitch said. "I can hardly wait! How long until we get there?"!

"Soon," Dwayne replied. "Now when the light turns green, make a right. Then—"

"There! It changed!"

"Mitch, you have to calm down some, or you're going to spook Stick. He's never met you before. Now just relax, and—"

"Holy Shit! This whole street is filled with nothing but strip clubs, as far as the eye can see!"

"Mitch!"

"What?"!

"Calm down and behave, or you'll have to wait in the car!"

"Okay-okay!" He took a deep breath. "I'm good."

"There's a spot." Dwayne pointed to it.

Mitch parked the car, and they walked inside.

"Good afternoon, sirs," a well dressed, clean-shaven man greeted them. "And welcome to The Hidden Treasure. May I take your coats for you?"

"No, thank you." Dwayne replied. "I believe we'll keep them."

"Very well. Enjoy yourselves."

Grasping the ornate wooden handrail, they started up the stairs to the main level. "Dude, it's hot as shit in here!" Mitch complained. "Why didn't you let that guy hold on to our coats?"

"Because, for executing the daunting task of putting your coat on a hanger and hanging it up for you, he would have expected a ten dollar tip. Do you have ten dollars to give him?"

"Ten dollars?"! Mitch exclaimed. "Hell, for ten bucks a pop, I'd hang up coats till my arms fell off!"

"Uh-huh."

"I'm not kidding! I'd be the best damn coat-hanger-upper person this joint has ever seen."

"I'm sure you would be. Now come on. I see Stick down at the end of the bar."

"Man, this place is awesome! Hey Dwayne, look up," Mitch said, peering up at the nude brunette performing on a brass pole, thirty feet in the air.

"Very nice, but I think you have a better chance of being hired as a coatroom attendant."

"No, dumbass! I don't mean I want to slide around naked on a pole; I was just telling you to check out the chick!"

Mitch continued to follow Dwayne with his head tilted back, unable to take his eyes off the beautiful woman. And in doing so, he didn't realize that they'd reached Dwayne's friend, and Dwayne had stopped.

"Hey Stick, how's—" Dwayne began to greet him, that is, until Mitch plowed into him. "Ooomph! Dammit, Mitch! Quit gawking at the girl and look where you're going!"

Stick snickered at the duo's gracelessness. Then he took a second look at Dwayne's companion. "Mitch! Mitch McMills. Is that really you?"!

"Steve!" Mitch grabbed Stick's hand and pulled him in for a manly handshake-shoulder-bump greeting. "How the hell have you been?"!

"You two know each other?"!

"Fuck yeah, we do!" Stick sniggered. "We were locked up together a few years back. Mitch was my cell buddy."

"Un-friggin-believable," Dwayne murmured, shaking his head. "Fine. You two go ahead and reminisce. I'm going to hit the restroom real quick."

"Uh-huh." Mitch turned his attention to Steve. "So, what have you been up to lately? How's Kathy?"

"It didn't work out. We just had too many problems. She and I got divorced about six months after I got out of jail."

"Oh. I'm sorry, dude."

"It's alright. I sort of figured that was going to be the case. We tried to make it work, writing and talking on the phone for a while, but there was just too much bad blood between us."

"You two sure used to get fucked up and beat the shit out of each other."

"Yeah. It seemed like the police were at our house almost every other weekend, and I was waking up in a jail cell as often as I was my own bedroom."

"That sucks."

"Eh, well, it was my own fault. I mean, we were doing every drug imaginable. Hell, if it could be shot, snorted, smoked, or swallowed, there was a good chance it was in our system. The crack might have been what killed us financially, but it was the time I freaked out on PCP that killed our marriage."

"Oh, I remember that night. You're talking about the night you killed her cat, right?"

"Yeah. The damn thing cornered me in the kitchen while I was hallucinating, and I thought it was a four-legged demon with horns, trying to kill me."

"So you decided to kill it, before it killed you."

"Yeah," he sighed and took a drink of his beer. "But when Kathy opened the microwave and saw her cat exploded inside of it, that was pretty much the end."

"I can see how that would have pissed her off."

"Yeah, it pissed the judge off, too! I got eighteen months in jail for that circus stunt! It ran concurrent with my other charges, but still, that was bullshit, man!"

"So you guys don't talk anymore?"

Stick bowed his head. "Not since they buried her."

"Buried her?"!

"Three months ago, today."

"How'd she die?"

"Shot up and fell out."

"No, shit! As experienced as she—"

"Experience don't mean shit, dude! She got ahold of some different stuff and overdosed. End of story."

"Damn. That's why I stay with the stuff I'm familiar with. I'll never OD."

Stick turned to Mitch. "You shouldn't say shit like that."

"Why? I won't ever fall out. I'm too careful."

"Dwayne and I have always been real superstitious about saying cocky shit like that."

"What do you mean?"

"Think about it. How many times have you heard people say they'll never do something? And how many times have those 'nevers' come true?"

Mitch got quiet.

The brief moment of contemplation soon turned in to several minutes of Mitch reflecting on his gruesome past.

"So," Stick said, "how did you meet Dwayne?"

Mitch didn't reply. He just kept staring off into the distance.

"Mitch?"

Still, no response.

"Mitch!"

"What?"

"What's wrong?"

"Nothing."

"I said, 'how'd you meet Dwayne?'"

"He and I woke up inside the same abandoned row house about six months ago, and we've been hanging out ever since."

"I had a feeling Dwayne was going to eventually end up living on the streets."

"Well, I don't know if I'd say he *lives* on the streets; he still spends a couple nights per week at his parents' house, but that doesn't always go so good."

"With his parents? You mean, with his mother."

"No, his dad lives there, too."

"Mitch, Dwayne's dad is *dead.*"

"Dead? He's not dead. What are you talking about?"

"Dude, trust me. He was killed a few years ago, in an explosion at the factory he used to work at. And as a result, Julie was awarded a ton of money."

"Who's Julie?"

"Dwayne's mom. Unfortunately though, to kill the pain of losing her husband, she turned to pills. And now Barry, the guy she buys her pills from, got her hooked on crack too – because he knows she's rich.

"Anyway, one day Barry decided he was going to *move in with them.*" Stick looked Mitch in the eye. "And that's just what he did... and that's when Dwayne went *ballistic.*"

"I can imagine."

"Yeah, it's really bad. Julie tries to justify it by telling people that Barry is her boyfriend. Barry, however, makes it clear to all his other lady friends that he is just living with one of his rich customers. It's all driving Dwayne crazy. But I guess it would drive me crazy, too, if I was forced to stand by and watch some asshole bleed *my* mother's bank account dry. Hell, Dwayne and Barry have gotten into fights so bad before, I mean, you just can't even imagine..."

"Now *that* I knew. I just assumed that the man Dwayne was fighting with was his father."

"Nope. Just a guy who lives there for free, charges his mom a fortune to keep her comatose, and beats on Dwayne for his own amusement."

"Well, I'll be damned," Mitch said.

"You'll be damned about what?" Dwayne asked, walking up behind them.

Mitch thought fast. "I'll be damned; you're finally back! Twenty minutes! Really? It takes you that long to piss?"!

"Take it easy on him, Mitch," Stick said. "He probably couldn't find his penis again."

Mitch burst out laughing.

"Screw you both! I've been talking to some people I used to go to school with."

Just then, a naked woman stepped between them. "Hey Stick, who are your friends?"

"This is Mitch, and that's Dwayne."

"Well, any friends of yours are friends of mine." She purred, putting her arms around their waists. "Either of you studs wanna join me in the back for some private fun?"

"Go ahead, Dwayne." Stick smiled. "Enjoy yourself. It'll give Mitch and I more time to catch up with each other."

"Pfft! Only if you talk really fast." Mitch chuckled. "As hot as she is, Dwayne will be done, and back out here in about two seconds!"

"Keep it up funny man, and you'll be *walking* home!" Dwayne exclaimed, turning to the beautiful woman. "And no, that's not why I'm declining your lovely offer."

"I know what the reason is." Stick reached for his wallet. "And don't worry about it. This one's on me."

"Perfect!" Candi shouted, grabbing Dwayne's ass.

"Whoa! No— I mean, I appreciate it. But I still can't." He removed her hand from his buttock.

"Seriously?" Stick and Mitch looked at each other. "Why not?"

"I don't want to say. You all will just bust my chops about it."

"No, we won't. No bullshit, man. What's wrong?"

Dwayne sighed. "Fine! Look, I've done some heinous things in my life. I've screwed up more times than I can count. Long story short, I got this girl, Jackie, and she's the best thing that ever happened to me. And I'd rather die than hurt her. And I know she'd never know. But I would. So, I'm sorry. I just can't."

Mitch, Stick, and Candi all looked at each other in silence. Then Candi turned to Dwayne. "Your Jackie is one very lucky girl. Guys like you are one in a million. I hope I find someone like you one day."

"Thanks. You're sweet."

"That's why they call me Candi." She winked at him.

"Mmmm... and I'd say they're most definitely correct," Mitch murmured.

"Okay, then. How about you, convict?" Stick gestured toward his ex-cellmate. "Are you dating anyone that—"

"Nope! I sure am not!" Mitch's eyes widened.

"Now, *that's* funny!" Dwayne seized his opportunity to exact an overdue retort. "I've never seen ol' Prissy Pants with a woman in my life! I'm not even sure he's straight!"

"What? No— I— You dick!"

"Is that right?"! Stick laughed. "Well, how about it, Mitch?"

"How about what?"

"Do you want to eat a piece of Candi?" the gorgeous temptress whispered in his ear.

Mitch's eyes sprung wide open. "Bye Dwayne! Just stay put! I'll be back in a little bit."

4

G iven how much time had elapsed since their last fix, to keep from getting violently ill, Mitch and Dwayne had no choice but to shoot up in the bathroom before they left the club.

After getting high, Dwayne elected to drive.

On the way back, he stopped off at a grocery store.

Pulling into an empty spot, he parked the car and tried to gather his thoughts. "Stay..." he murmured, turning toward Mitch, his eyes falling half closed, "here. I'll be right back."

But Mitch was incapable of replying, for he had already nodded off in the passenger seat. Once again, he was teetering on the brink of a lethal overdose.

Inside the store, Dwayne selected an item, paid for it, and walked back out to his car.

He secured his purchase in the back seat, drove to the abandoned row house in which they had awoken that morning, and pulled to the side of the road. "Alright, you gotta get out."

"Huh?" Mitch grunted, raising his eyelids just enough to reveal his pinpointed pupils.

"Get out of the car, before you make me late!" Dwayne reached over and opened his door for him. "Go find a bench or something."

Mitch eased himself out of the vehicle, shuffled his feet a few steps, and then plopped down in the middle of the sidewalk.

"Good 'nuf," Dwayne said, driving away, his door closing on its own volition.

5

rriving at his mother's house, Dwayne parked next to Barry's prize sports car. His first thought was to thrust his door open into it. But he refrained.

Walking up to the front door, he turned the knob and tiptoed inside, hoping no one would hear him.

"Hello," Julie said from where she lay sprawled out on the sofa.

Dwayne closed his eyes and sighed. "Hi, mom."

"How wuz zhur day, dear?"

"Fine. Where's Barry?"

"Heezh in nah kitchen... makings me a drink."

Dwayne stomped into the kitchen, snatched the gin and tonic out of Barry's hands, and dumped it into the sink. "She doesn't need any alcohol on top of whatever else she's on right now! She can't even talk as it is!" He slammed the empty glass down on the countertop and stormed upstairs.

Rushing down the hall to his bedroom, he grabbed a nice button-up shirt, dress pants, dark socks, and boxers, and threw everything onto the bed. His eyes darted to the digital clock on his nightstand. "Shit!" He hurried off to the bathroom.

Meanwhile, Barry's anger festered. Hell-bent on avenging himself, he walked over to the closet, slid the coats to the left, and retrieved the baseball bat from the back. (Julie had hidden it there after Dwayne's dad died, to defend herself against potential intruders. Unfortunately, Barry also knew where it was.)

In a satanic state of mind, he crept up the stairs and down the hall with his weapon. As the sound of the shower became louder, his diabolical grin grew.

Without making a sound, the psychopath walked into the bathroom, positioned himself beside the shower, and reared the bat back.

But just as he began to propel it forward, the bathroom mirror caught his eye. He paused to write something on its steamy surface.

Then he drew the bat back by his ear again and swung as hard as he could, striking the unsuspecting young man on the opposite side of the shower curtain with unspeakable force.

Satisfied with his retaliatory attack, Barry headed back downstairs, chuckling to himself as his victim lay on the floor of the tub, writhing in agony.

When Dwayne was finally able to stand up, he opened the shower curtain and peered over at the writing on the mirror, which read, "Learn some manners."

In spite of his aching arm, Dwayne managed to put on his underwear, socks, and pants in a relatively short amount of time.

His shirt, however, wasn't going to be as easy. After inserting his one good arm through the sleeve, he had no choice but to take a deep breath and force his injured arm back to find the armhole. "Ahh!" he cried out.

As soon as he was done getting ready, he dashed out of his bedroom and scurried down the steps. Half way down the stairway though, he stopped in his tracks and uttered, "Shit!"

Running back up to his room, Dwayne squatted down beside his bed and felt around under his mattress.

At first, he didn't feel anything! His stomach got hot, and his heart began to pound.

Then his thumb bumped into something. "Whew!" He breathed a sigh of relief.

Grabbing what he'd located, he stuffed the item into his pocket and hurried off to his dinner engagement.

6

When Dwayne arrived at his destination, he retrieved his package from the back seat, walked up to the house, and rang the bell.

The door was soon opened by a nicely dressed middle-aged woman. "Good evening, Dwayne." She smiled. "Come on in. Make yourself at home."

"Thank you, Mrs. Ramsey. How are you tonight?"

"I'm doing great. How about you?"

"I'm well. Here ma'am, I brought you something." He handed her a flat box.

"Well now, what's this?" she asked, opening it. "Oh my, strawberry cheesecake! Dwayne, this looks delicious, honey, but you didn't have to bring dessert."

"No, but I wanted too. I'm certain it will pale in comparison to your phenomenal culinary talents, but I've always been taught it's impolite to show up as a guest to dinner empty-handed."

"My stars! You, sir, never cease to amaze me. And thank you for the lovely compliment. That was very sweet of you. Please excuse me for a minute while I put your cheesecake in the refrigerator."

"Certainly. Take your time."

"Cheesecake?"! A jovial man's voice could be heard coming from the family room. "Did I hear someone say 'cheesecake'?"

"Oh, Clark! Honestly!" Mrs. Ramsey laughed. "That was selective hearing at its finest."

"It's a special gift that we husbands have, Joleen."

"Uh-huh. I hear ya, old man. Now get out of my way until dinner's ready. Go say 'hi' to Dwayne. Take him to the game room or something for ten minutes. Maybe he'll be nice and let you win a game of billiards."

"Okay. I'll— Hey! What do you mean, 'maybe he'll *let* me win'? I shoot a good game of pool."

"Whatever you say, dear." She kissed him on the cheek as she hustled by. "Now scoot!"

Brushing off her wisecrack, Clark made his way to the foyer to meet Dwayne. "Hey son, how ya' doing? Jackie's still upstairs primping. You know how women are."

"I heard that!" Joleen hollered from two rooms away.

"And she picks on me about *my* selective hearing." He rolled his eyes. "Would you like to shoot a game of pool, or just kick your feet up in a recliner and watch the idiot box for a spell?"

The mere thought of playing pool made him cringe, given how his arm ached. "I'd just like to watch a little television if that's alright with you."

"Sure. Have a seat anywhere you like."

"Thank you, sir." He eased himself into the closest chair. Just then, he got a whiff of something. "Mmmm, what smells so good?"

"Good as in 'food'? Or good as in 'weird'?"

"Good as in 'food.' But what do you mean by 'weird'?"

"The food that smells so good is the beef stew that Joleen's been slow cooking in the crock pot since this morning, and the weirdness you smell is one of those darn incense sticks she's got burning in here somewhere. I hate those blessed things."

"Oh, I'm familiar with incense sticks. My mother used to burn them too. I think her favorite was a scent called 'summer sunset.' No, wait. Maybe it was 'morning dew.'"

"That would be fine if Joleen purchased something with a pretty name like that. But Dwayne, I swear! The last thing that woman brought home smelled like it ought to have been called, 'monkey's ass!'"

Dwayne burst out laughing.

Clark raised his eyebrows. "I'm serious."

Just then, a petite young lady emerged from around the corner, wearing an adorable sundress. "What's so funny?" she asked.

"Oh my!" Dwayne popped out of his recliner, gaping at her long dark hair and big brown eyes. Swallowing hard, he tried to suppress the nervousness he still felt upon initially seeing her.

Jackie smiled, bit her lower lip, and then glanced downward before looking back up at him.

"Jackie, you're— you're so pretty," Dwayne murmured in an airy voice of sincerity. "I mean, like... breathtaking."

Jackie looked into his eyes and whispered, "I love you."

Dwayne's stomach filled with butterflies. "I—" his voice cracked. Embarrassed by the funny squeak that just escaped his larynx, he cleared his throat and tried again. "I love you too."

She touched her hand to his cheek and smiled. "You can stay here and talk to daddy if you like. I'm going to go to the kitchen see if mom needs any help."

"Okay."

Jackie couldn't have been gone for more than a minute or so when Joleen hollered, "Dinner's ready!"

"Yes!" Clark jumped out of his recliner. "My two most favorite words in the world!"

Convening in the dining room, Joleen enjoyed watching the men drink in the mixture of intoxicating aromas as they entered.

Even the table, itself, was a masterpiece: lacey trim embellished the outer edge of a fitted tablecloth; fresh, fragrant flowers composed the handmade centerpiece; and each place setting boasted warm buttermilk biscuits, a crisp garden salad, and a generous helping of beef stew—all of which was accompanied by a glass of red wine.

"Whoa!" Dwayne gasped. "Mrs. Ramsey, you've outdone yourself. I'm speechless."

"Speechless is fine," Joleen replied. "People aren't supposed to talk with their mouth full, anyway. So sit down and dig in."

"You don't have to tell me twice," Clark said, plopping into the closest chair.

"Huh-umm." Joleen cleared her throat in order to get her husband's attention. And when he looked at her, she nodded toward Dwayne, who was performing the old-fashioned custom of pulling Jackie's chair out for her.

"So, did you get lucky when selecting your dessert?" Joleen asked. "Or did Jackie tell you that strawberry cheesecake is my favorite?"

"She didn't tell me. I made a mental note of how much you and Mr. Ramsey enjoyed the Sykesville Strawberry Festival a while back. And when I was at the store, the bakery person recommended their cheesecake. So I guess you could say I merged the two thoughts."

"Well, you did a fine job. I can't believe you remembered me raving about the strawberry festival. That's been ages ago. You'll have to teach Clark how to make mental notes like that."

"What are you talking about?" Clark asked. "I have a great memory."

"Yeah, when it comes to how many home runs a player catches, you have a great memory. But not when it comes to things that matter."

"Players don't catch home runs, dear. They hit them."

"I think he missed the point, mom." Jackie giggled.

"No, he didn't. Your father's very sneaky. He's just trying to avoid the question. Watch, I'll test him."

"Test me? But I don't want to be tested! Since when did this become 'pick-on-Clark night'?"

"When's our Anniversary, Clark?" Joleen asked in a monotone voice, resting her elbow on the table, and her chin in her hand.

The poor man looked hopeless.

"Or how about my birthday?" She fired off a second inquiry.

"Who holds the record for most consecutive games played in baseball?" Dwayne asked, coming to his rescue.

Clark's eyes lit up. "Calvin Edward Ripken Jr. Better known as Cal. Born 1960. The shortstop for the Baltimore Orioles was the American league's most valuable player in 1983 and 1991. He broke Lou Gehrig's streak of 2,130 consecutive games in 1995, and ended his own streak in 1998 at 2,632 consecutive games."

Joleen rolled her eyes. "Amazing," she muttered, taking a sip of coffee.

"Thanks for bailing me out of that one, Dwayne," Clark said.

"No problem. I had to choose between throwing you a life preserver or finish sinking your ship by joining in and asking you something crazy, like when *my* birthday is."

"Well, thank you. I was starting to take on quite a bit of water, there."

"Next week," Joleen said out of the blue.

"What, mom?" Jackie asked.

"Next week," she repeated.

"What about next week?"

"Dwayne's birthday is next week."

"No, it's not. It's... it's... Hey, I don't think you ever told me when your birthday is. *Is* your birthday next week, Dwayne?"

Dwayne peered over at Joleen. "Now how in the world did you know that?"

"Because I'm a mother. And mothers know everything."

"So, it *is* next week?"! Jackie's eyes widened. "But sweetheart, how am I supposed to buy you a birthday present if I don't know when your birthday is?"

"You don't need to buy me anything for my birthday. Presents are most special when they're given as a complete surprise, anyway. Don't worry about it."

Jackie bowed her head. "Well, yeah... I guess so." She pushed an abandoned pea through a puddle of broth on her plate. "But who does that?"

"I do."

"Huh?"

"I do," Dwayne repeated, reaching into his pocket, pulling out the skinny white box he'd retrieved from under his mattress.

"Is this for me?"! Her eyes burst wide open. "But why?"!

"Like I said, regular people only give gifts on special occasions. But I like to give gifts just to say 'you're special.'"

"How sweet," she whispered.

"How dear." Joleen smiled.

"How ingenious!" Clark shouted, shattering the tender moment. "The boy's a genius! That means he's off the hook! He doesn't have to remember any of those exact dates that you girls get all goofy about, because he's covered his bases by buying presents randomly throughout the year! What a great idea!"

"You're hopeless, Clark." Joleen shook her head.

Jackie unwrapped her present. "A necklace! Mom, look! It's beautiful!"

"Wow, that *is* pretty! I love the heart pendant."

"That was very nice of you, son." Clark winked at him.

"Put it on, honey." Joleen looked around the room for her camera. "And Dwayne, you come over here and stand beside her. I want to take your picture."

Dwayne walked over and stood beside her.

Joleen looked through the lens. "Okay, say 'lovey-ducks'!"

"Say what?" Dwayne laughed just as she took the picture.

Joleen looked down at the screen display on the back of her camera. "Dwayne! What's wrong with you? Your eyes are closed and your face is all scrunched up like you got a horsefly stuck up your nose. Now smile right."

"I'm sorry, Mrs. Ramsey, but I was expecting you to say, 'say cheese.' You caught me off guard. Okay, I'm ready now."

Dwayne smiled nicely, and Joleen took another picture. "Got it!" She grinned. "Okay, you can go back and sit down now."

"Oh no he can't—not until I give him a kiss for my present," Jackie said, grabbing ahold of his arm.

"OWW!!" Dwayne cried out, dropping to his knees.

"Oh my God! Dwayne! What's wrong?"! Joleen stooped down beside him, placing her hand on his back.

Jackie cupped her hand over her mouth, her eyes widening in horror.

Clark sprung from his chair and raced to the young man's side. "Just keep taking deep breaths, son. Do you want us to call 9-1-1?"

"No." He squeezed his eyes shut and clenched his teeth.

"Can you tell us what's wrong?"

"I hurt my arm," he replied in a wispy voice.

"How?"

"I— I hurt it." He tried making it to his feet.

"I know you hurt it. But *how* did you hurt it? What happened?" Joleen asked, helping him stand up.

Dwayne wiped his eyes, cleared his throat, and collected himself as fast as he could. "Aw, you know how guys are, Mrs. Ramsey. We're always doing stuff, where we end up getting hurt."

"I know, but—"

"Pssst!" Clark got his wife's attention and shot her a look to make her stop probing. "Can you make it back over to your chair, Dwayne?"

"Yeah." He hobbled over to the recliner and sat down. Then his eyes drifted about the room until he located his girlfriend. "Jackie?" He whispered, licking his dry lips.

"Yes, sweetheart! What is it?"

"Jackie, can you come here a minute?"

"Oh, sure." She hurried to his side.

Everyone in the room held their breath, wondering what he was about to say.

"Jackie." Dwayne forced a smile to ease the tension. "You promised me a kiss a minute ago, and I still haven't gotten it."

"Oh, Dwayne!" She giggled, breathing a sigh of relief, giving him his kiss.

Then Clark motioned for Joleen to join him in the kitchen.

Within seconds, Clark returned with an ice pack. "Jackie, your mother needs you in the kitchen a minute. Would you mind giving her a hand?"

"Oh sure. I'll be right back, Dwayne. You just sit there and take it easy."

Once Jackie left, all became still.

The two men were alone.

Dwayne sat in the recliner, and Clark on the sofa.

First, they just looked at each other.

Then Clark eased himself forward until his butt reached the edge of the cushion, rested his elbows on his knees, and interlocked his fingers. But he still, he didn't speak.

Dwayne couldn't take the silence any longer. "Mrs. Ramsey's right, you know."

"About what?" Clark asked.

"About you being sneaky."

"What makes you say that?"

"Because, less than a minute after I collapse to the floor, you manage to empty the room of two women I scared to death; and you expect me not to notice. You're slick, sir. I'll give you that."

"Apparently not slick enough, though. I get caught every time."

Dwayne smiled, leaving an opening in their conversation. And Clark took advantage of it. "Is it broken?" he asked.

"What? Oh, I didn't—"

"Dwayne." Clark closed his eyes and raised his hand. "Stop."

"No, really. See, what happened was—"

"Dwayne! No."

"What?"

"Don't try to bullshit me. I may suck at being sneaky, but I can smell a bullshit story from a mile away. Okay?"

"Okay."

"Now Dwayne, we've built a relationship based on many honorable values. And one of those values is 'trust.'"

"Right. And...?"

"And I'm not exactly an advocate of keeping secrets, but we men have to stick together. Sometimes, we'll learn stuff about each other that's simply none of Joleen or Jackie's business. And quite frankly, what happened to your arm is simply none of their business. They would just get all worried and make a fuss.

"And as men, it's our job to minimize their worry and to ensure they have harmony in their lives. Because, when the woman's life is kept harmonious, the man's life remains peaceful. Right?"

"Right." Dwayne cracked a little grin.

"So, you see?" Clark slowed his speech. "It's simply none of their business."

"I understand."

"But Dwayne...?" He looked him square in the eye.

"Yes, Mr. Ramsey?"

"You've become like a son to me. And I'm *making* it *my* business. Now, whatever I see under that shirt sleeve of yours goes nowhere. Nothing gets said outside of this room. You don't tell the girls. I won't tell the girls. But I *am* going to look at it and take care of you. Understand?"

"Yes, sir."

Dwayne swallowed hard and raised his shirt sleeve, revealing a grotesque bruise containing blotches of deep purple.

He waited on Clark to freak out, but he didn't. He didn't even flinch. All he said was, "Let me see you wriggle your fingers."

Dwayne successfully moved his fingers up and down, and curled them.

"How about your thumb?

It also checked out.

"How about your arm? Can you bend it?"

Forgetting about his needle tracks, Dwayne bent his arm, exposing a long row of marks on the underside of his forearm.

Realizing what he'd done, he hurriedly straightened it back out.

But even then, Clark remained calm.

By this time, Dwayne's mind was bursting at the seams with unanswered questions: Did he not notice the tracks because of all the bruising? Or did he see the evidence of his drug addiction, and just not say anything? But why? How could he not say anything?

Clark inhaled a deep breath, held it for a second, and then exhaled it through his mouth, blowing out his cheeks. "Well, I'm by no means a doctor, Dwayne, but I don't think it's broken. It's going to be stiff and sore for a few weeks, but you should be fine." Then he slid his butt back into the sofa and began watching television again.

Dwayne was speechless. He just stared at him for a few moments, until finally, he couldn't take it any longer. "And...?"! he blurted out.

"And *what*, Dwayne? Look, I'm sorry, but I don't have a toy to give you for behaving like a good little boy during your visit to Dr. Ramsey's pretend medical practice, but if you go out to the kitchen, Joleen might have a cookie for you."

Dwayne looked at the man like he had three heads. "Huh! No, that's not what I—"

"Oh, and on your way back, bring me another glass of wine. I read somewhere that a glass of wine a day is supposed to be good for us old folks, so I figure I'll *double* the benefits by having two, right?"

"No. Uh, I mean— Yeah I don't know aren't you gonna bug me about how I screwed up my arm?"! he said without pausing between sentences.

"Nope," Clark replied, "but what I am going to do, is insist that you take the bottle of ibuprofen we have up in the medicine cabinet home with you when you leave tonight. Read the dosage instructions on the side of the bottle, then take twice that; it won't hurt you. It'll help reduce the pain and swelling. God knows Mr. Blackston probably doesn't keep any in the house."

"Mr. Blackston?" Dwayne murmured, knowing the name sounded familiar. Then his eyes became humongous. "Mr. Blackston! Mr. *Barry* Blackston! How do you know Barry? Better yet, how do you know Barry lives with—" Dwayne's mind surged into overdrive. Did Clark know about him living on the streets? Did he know his mom? Or about his past?

Suddenly, he felt sick.

"Aw, shit!" Clark dug around next to him in the sofa. "Here! Take this ice pack and put it on your arm; I went to the kitchen to get it for you, brought it back here with me, and then forgot all about it. See, that's what happens when you get old."

"Nice try," Dwayne said.

"Nice try, *what*?"

"Nice try on avoiding my question, Mr. Slick. Now, how do you know Barry?"

"Dammit! I don't know who's more perceptive, you or Joleen. Alright, fine, Barry is one of my customers. He comes in to the garage to have his car worked on all the time."

"Why's he there so much?"

"Because he drag races on weekends, and ever since he had us put a NOS system in his car, it feels like he's there every damn day."

"That must suck. I can at least try to stay out of my house as much as possible, but you can't stay away from your work."

"You got that right. And Dwayne, you know me. I'm an easy going guy, right?"

"Oh, sure, Mr. Ramsey."

"Live and let live, I always say."

"Uh-huh."

"I mean, shit, I've even been trying to watch my fuckin' language lately."

"And you're doing a darn good job of it, sir!" Dwayne chuckled.

"But sometimes, I just want to shove that asshole's head in a vice, draw it down tight on his skull, and jam a few screwdrivers in his eye sockets."

Dwayne's face lost all expression. He'd never heard Clark talk that way before. "Mr. Ramsey, that has got to be the wickedest thing I've ever heard in my life."

"Wicked, huh?" Clark repeated the word from where he sat on the sofa. Then he forced a stern expression and stuck out his chest. "Yup, that's my middle name. Clark 'Wicked' Ramsey!"

"I see," Dwayne replied, raising his eyebrows. "Well, let me ask you this, Dr. Wicked, how'd—"

"Oh, hey! I *really* like that!"

"Like what?"

"Being called 'Dr. Wicked'!"

"That's nice." Dwayne ignored the digression. "So, how does Mrs. Ramsey know when my birthday is?"

Clark smiled and looked directly at Dwayne. "You happen to be dating our daughter." He pointed to himself, touching his finger to his chest. "*My* daughter. Daddy's little princess. Son, I check out anyone she spends a significant amount of time with."

"Check them out? How?"

Clark picked up the television remote and began channel surfing. "On the internet. Joleen belongs to one of those background check websites. All she has to do is enter someone's name, and it tells her everything about them."

For the second time in as many minutes, Dwayne felt sick to his stomach. "*Everything* about them?" He gulped hard, his heart racing.

"Yup. Everything," Clark replied, never looking away from the television.

"So, you know all about my history, my family, my—"

"Yup." He cut him off. "And the rehabs you've been to, your criminal record, the works. Hell, I can almost tell you when you last wiped your ass! Ain't technology great?"!

"So, if you know all those horrible things about me, why are you still so nice to me? Why haven't you forbidden Jackie from dating me?"

Now *that* question got Mr. Ramsey's attention. He clicked off the television and turned toward Dwayne. "Many years ago, there was a young man who got wrapped up in the same things that are weighing on you right now. He couldn't hold a job, he had problems with alcohol and drugs, and he was in and out of jail more times than he could count.

"Nearly everyone who saw him judged him and deemed him worthless. But deep down, he was actually a very nice person. Not just a nice person, but a righteous, respectable, good-hearted person. A God-fearing individual who just had a lot of bad things happen to him. And those things led him to make some very poor decisions in life. But in spite of all that, there was one man who gave him a chance when no one else would. One man who believed in him when no one else did. And because of that one man, he managed to accomplish the impossible: he began to believe in himself. He grew strong and became confident. He got off the smack, cleaned up his act, and learned a trade. Ultimately, he turned his whole life around. He even ended up marrying the daughter of the man who believed in him, and they lived happily ever after. And do you know what, Dwayne?

"No. What?"

"That woman's father is Walt, my father-in-law; and the young man he believed in, is *me*."

Goosebumps streamed down Dwayne's arms. "No way! Really?"!

"Yes. And now, the time has come."

"The time has come for what?"

"The time has come for me to pay it forward. Dwayne, you have a heart of gold. You make Jackie happier than I ever hoped she could be. I said you're like a son to me, and God as my witness, I have never spoken a truer word. You have some issues to work out, I know. Some of them, quite serious. But look into my eyes when I say this."

Dwayne sat erect in his chair and looked into Clark's eyes.

"I believe in you, son. I believe in you, and I welcome you into our family with open arms. It's all up to you now. And you know what I mean. Look, you can do it. I'm behind you all the way, and I'm here for whatever you need, okay?"

"I... I don't know what to say, Mr. Ramsey." Dwayne's eyes welled up.

"You don't have to say anything. Actions speak louder than words. And if you ever decide that our little buddy, Barry, needs his attitude adjusted, you just let me know. I got some six-foot-tall, 300 pound friends down at the shop that would be more than happy to show him what it's like to be on the wrong end of an unfair fight." Clark pointed his remote at the television and clicked it back on. "I'm not insinuating he had anything to do with your injury, of course."

"Pffft, no, of course not." Dwayne rolled his eyes.

"I'm just saying, if you need me for anything at all, don't hesitate to ask."

"Thank you, sir. That means a lot to me."

"No problem. Now go get the girls and tell them they can come back in. If they get to asking questions, we'll just tell them 'it's just a bruise, and you'll be fine.' And then I'll change the subject really fast."

"Um, no offense, Mr. Slick, but let's leave the crafty changing of subjects to me, shall we?"

"Smartass!" Clark chuckled.

"What if they ask us what took so long?"

"Eh, we'll just say we talked about me borrowing your car tomorrow."

"We're gonna *lie* to them?"

"No, I really *do* need to borrow your car tomorrow, that is, if you don't mind. My car has to stay at the shop overnight because we're only allowed to work on our personal vehicles at certain times, and I won't be able to tear mine apart and have it back together in just one day."

"Oh, sure. You can borrow it anytime you need to. It's going to embarrass you though, because it smokes a lot. And it may leave you stranded somewhere, so be prepared. And if it makes a bunch of clicking noises when you turn the key, just keep trying. It should eventually start... hopefully."

"Okay. Thanks for the heads-up. And now it won't be a lie when we tell the girls that we talked about me borrowing your car tomorrow."

"Perfect. Okay, I'll go get them. Besides, I still want my cookie for not giving Dr. Wicked a hard time during my doctor's appointment." Dwayne sniggered on his way to the kitchen.

7

On his way home, the minor withdrawal symptoms that Dwayne had been fighting off at Jackie's house came on full-force, catapulting him into an ill world of intolerable suffering.

It was as if a cave existed in the pit of his soul, and in that cave, there dwelled a demon. And as long as Dwayne constantly fed the demon's insatiable appetite, the omnipotent, sadistic beast would lie dormant.

Currently, however, Dwayne's demon was emerging from its cave, feeling ravenous and enraged.

Annoying cravings and anxiety were evolving into profuse sweating, cold chills, and stabbing abdominal cramps.

There wasn't much time.

He had to pull over, preferably into the lot of a fast food restaurant, where there would be a restroom.

Dwayne's stomach began rolling and churning.

He wasn't sure whether he was going to vomit or have diarrhea, but the one thing he was sure of was that *something* was soon going to explode.

Just then, he saw a large building up ahead with cars in the parking lot. As he continued to drive, the sign out front became legible. It read, "Adaram Industries, Inc."

He turned into Lot B, the parking area designated for those working the third shift. There, he wasn't sticking out like a sore thumb by parking along the side of the road. But on the other hand, he had no access to a bathroom.

It would have to do.

Pulling between two vehicles, he turned off his lights, flung open his door, and proceeded to projectile vomit.

Bile, mucus, and partially digested chunks of beef all hit the blacktop at once, splattering everywhere.

Following the ferocious expectoration, he knew there would be a very short-lived period of relief, during which time, he needed to use to get high again.

He unbuckled his belt and unbuttoned his pants to get to the double-layered flap of material that covered his zipper. Shoving the tip of his pinkie into the cut he had made in the overlap, he accessed the tiny pocket that had resulted from making the incision.

From that miniature secret compartment, Dwayne extracted a $20 bag of dope. It was just what he needed to turn his abominable flulike symptoms into the most pleasurable, euphoric feeling in the world.

Reaching into the back, he grabbed a water bottle off the floor; and from the glove compartment, he retrieved a lighter and a cotton swab. Then he stuck his hand under the dash and curled his fingers upward to access a cubbyhole, where he kept a tablespoon and a syringe hidden.

Dwayne removed the cap from the bottle of water, submerged the needle, and pulled back on the plunger to partially fill it.

Then he plucked some of the cotton from the end of the swab, rolled it around between his thumb and index finger to form a dense ball (about the size of an apple seed), and set it on his thigh.

Very carefully, he dumped the diminutive baggie of heroin onto the spoon, discarded the baggie, and picked up the syringe.

Sweat streamed down his face.

Pushing through the pain, he depressed the plunger, shooting a thin stream of water into the miniscule mound of powder, instantaneously dissolving it.

Moving with the utmost care to avoid spilling the precious solution, he brought the syringe to his mouth, grasped the plastic end with his teeth, and picked up the lighter. "Flick." He raked his thumb across the top of it, turning the little metal cylinder.

But it didn't light.

"Flick." He tried a second time. Once again, nothing happened. "Shit!" Dwayne shook the lighter. "Come on!" He tried again. It ignited that time, and he positioned the flame under the spoon, instantly bringing the mixture to a boil.

As soon as the dealer's added cut burned off, he picked the ball of cotton up off his leg and placed it in the center of the spoon to soak up the infusion.

Sweat dripped from his nose, yet he was freezing cold.

Dwayne snatched the syringe out of his mouth, inserted the point of the needle into the cotton ball, and pulled back on the plunger, drawing the liquid up into the cylindrical cavity.

Suddenly, a "shiver" thundered through his body with such force, he dropped his spoon just as it emptied. "Oh, God!" He gasped.

Next, he held the needle upright and flicked it twice to bring any air bubbles to the top. Then he pressed the plunger just enough to expel the air.

"So c-c-c-cold!" His voice quivered as he wrestled with his cuff, trying to unbutton his shirtsleeve.

Typically, he experienced no difficulty in locating a vein to use. In fact, normally there would be several big ones from which he could choose.

But given the bruising that existed, that was not the case tonight. "Fuh-fuh-fuh-fuck!!" He gawked at his swollen, discolored appendage.

Thinking he saw a vein, he held his breath in an attempt to hold the needle still, despite how badly his body was trembling.

Unable to wait any longer, he lowered the point to his skin and pushed, driving the hollow metal spike into his flesh.

Hoping the tip hit its target, he paused to perform the test: leaving the needle in his arm, he repositioned his thumb and index finger, and extracted the plunger a quarter inch.

Aspiring to see a bright red swirl appear, he examined it.

But the mixture remained clear. "Shit!" he growled, feeling a bout of diarrhea gurgling in his gut.

Outraged by his contusion's uncanny ability to camouflage his blood vessels, he yanked the needle out and shoved it back in a different spot.

Once again, he repositioned his fingers and tugged on the plunger. Blood gushed up inside the needle and mixed with the liquid. Without hesitation, he ejected the solution from the syringe, sending it into his bloodstream.

"Ahhh." Dwayne closed his eyes as a warm sensation made its way out to his extremities.

His abdomen no longer hurt.

His cold chills, sweating, and chattering teeth miraculously disappeared.

Sheer euphoria filled every cell in his body.

He didn't have a care in the world. Even his arm felt good.

All that was uncontrollable now was the size of his smile, which grew in proportion to the intensity of the bitter taste he had in the back of his throat from shooting up.

Then came the final, most dangerous stage of his high: the 'pins-and-needles.' From head to toe, Dwayne's entire body tingled with ten times the dopamine of a normal person, enabling him to experience a level of pleasure that's impossible for regular human beings to even imagine.

Unfortunately though, reaching this paralyzing, zombielike state also meant that he was close to overdosing—right there in his car—in the parking lot of Adaram Industries.

But for now, that didn't matter. Nothing mattered. For the demon had been fed.

8

Early the next morning, a security guard for Adaram Industries found Dwayne in his car. He woke him up and made him leave.

Dwayne headed back to his house to get a shower.

This time, no one else was home. "Thank God." He breathed a sigh of relief.

Dwayne brushed his teeth, combed his hair, and spritzed on some cologne.

And although he didn't have to steal or pawn anything to cop dope that afternoon, he put on a suit and darted back out the door.

Hopping in his car, he tilted the rearview mirror downward to check himself out one last time before leaving.

Giving a little grin, Dwayne put on his sunglasses and turned the key. "Click-click-click-click-click."

"Dammit!" he bellowed, repetitively stomping the accelerator to the floor. "Start, you son of a bitch!" He turned the key again.

Smoke poured out the exhaust pipe, but at least it started.

"Yes!" He drove off.

9

"Good morning." The woman at the information desk greeted Dwayne. "Can I help you?"

"Yes, ma'am," he replied. "What do I need to do to be able to use a computer?"

"You just need a library card. Do you have one?"

"I used to, but I have no idea where it is now."

"That's okay." She handed a slip of paper. "Just fill this out, and I'll issue you a new one."

"Aw, cool. Thanks."

Dwayne wrote down his name, address, and telephone number; and handed it back to her so she could enter his information into the system.

"Okay, honey." She smiled. "Now I just need you to give me a password you want to use, and you'll be all set."

"A password for what?"

"When you sit down at the computer, it will ask you for your user ID number—which is the number on the card I'm going to give you—and a password. Try to pick something that you can remember."

"Oh, okay. Let's make it 'Jackie.'"

"Oops. I should have told you, it has to be at least eight characters long, and contain at least one number."

"Hmmm." He squeezed one eye shut as he thought. "How about, 'Jackie22'?"

"Sounds good to me. Now, once you login to a computer, you'll have up to two hours to use it. Printed pages are ten cents apiece, and the printer's located right over there." She pointed at it.

"Okay. Thanks for all your help."

"My pleasure."

Dwayne walked over to an empty workstation, entered his login and password, and opened Internet Explorer. In the box that appeared, he typed "sample resumes," and hit the "enter" key.

But every single one of the results that popped up mentioned something along the lines of, "Download over one hundred resume formats for only $19.99."

"Screw that!" he muttered, hitting the 'back' button. "Let's try something a little different."

This time he typed, "Free sample resume, young person."

Dwayne scanned the updated search results. "Bingo, baby!"

"Shhh!" an old man sitting nearby hushed him.

"Sorry," he whispered, giving him a polite wave.

Then he perused some of the sites to get an idea of what a resume for a person who didn't have much work experience was supposed to look like.

Mimicking his favorite format, he created a very nice looking resume, fed the machine a dollar, printed out ten copies, and proceeded to his next stop.

10

Parking in front of a large one-story building, Dwayne grabbed his resumes and headed inside.

The woman on the other side of the counter was on the phone. She covered the receiver and whispered, "I'll be right with you."

"Take your time," Dwayne said, gawking at the walls of the lobby, which were plastered with posters of scantily dressed women bending over car hoods, posing in provocative positions, and washing vehicles in wet t-shirts.

Finally, he heard the lady say, "Sorry about that." She hung up the phone and approached the counter. "Can I help you?"

"Yes," Dwayne replied. "Is Mr. Ramsey available?"

"Hold on. I'll check." She walked to a steel-framed glass door behind her desk and stopped. Instead of opening it with her hands (like a normal person would do), the skinny little woman turned around, bent over, and began pushing it open with her *butt*.

The whooping and hollering that ensued from the mechanics on the opposite side of the door was deafening.

Finally, she managed to crack it open just far enough to be able to turn around and face them. "Clark!" she screamed, swiping her bangs out of her eyes.

He peered over an old Pontiac that he was working on. "Yeah?"

"Clark! Come up front!" She waved him in. "You got a vis—"

"Bang!" The door slammed shut, catapulting her frail physique a good eight feet back inside, sending her stumbling about. "Damn, that thing!" The possessed-looking receptionist whirled around toward Dwayne. "He's on his way!"

Dwayne took a couple steps back from the counter. "Thank you. Are you, uh... feeling alright?"

"Am I alright?"! Her eyes became huge. "No, I'm not alright! And do you know why? Because one of those numbnuts cranked up the pressure on the door's closing arm yesterday! So now, whenever I need to open it, I gotta smash my ass all up against the glass; and everyone on the other side gets their jollies by watching it squish around as I struggle to get through the friggin' doorway!"

Just then, Clark entered.

"Was it you?"! she yelled, thrusting her extended pointer finger in his face, holding it an inch from his nose.

"Was *what* me?"

"The door closing arm! Was it you that turned it up, to make it so I can't open the door anymore?"!

"No." He chuckled, pushing her finger to the side.

"Are you sure it wasn't you?"!

"Yes, I'm sure."

"Do you know who did it?"

"Yup."

"Really? Who?"!

"I'm not telling you." Clark turned his attention to Dwayne. "Good morning, son. You look sharp. Why are you all dressed up?"

"Because of what you told me last night. You're right, 'It's all up to me, now.' So, I dressed nicely, went to the library, created a resume, printed out a bunch of copies, and now I'm going to hit the streets."

"You're going to *hit the streets*, huh?" Clark grinned.

"Yes, sir. While you're using my car over the next couple days, I'm going to walk to businesses around town and apply for jobs."

"That's great!" Clark looked at the papers in his hand. "Are they your resumes?"

"Yes. Would you like to see one?"

"Sure." He took a minute to critique it. "Very impressive. I especially like the format."

"Thank you. You can use my car as long as you like. The keys are in the ignition. Well, I'd better get going if—"

"Hold on. Just sit tight a second. I'll be right back." Clark retrieved an imitation leather folder from the supply closet. "Here you go."

"What's that for?"

"To put your resumes in. It looks a lot more professional than carrying your pens and paper around loose in your hand."

"Crap! I didn't think about bringing a pen!"

"That's alright. I put two in there for you. That way, you'll have a spare if you leave one lay somewhere."

"Awesome! Thanks, Mr. Ramsey."

"Yup. You have yourself a nice day now, 'ya hear?"

"Yes, sir!" Dwayne smiled. "You too. Bye!"

11

"I'm all finished filling out the application, ma'am," Dwayne said, making good eye contact with the assistant manager of the grocery store. "Do you have a stapler?"

"I sure do," she replied. "Here you go."

"Thanks. And what did you say your name was again?"

"Rhonda."

"Thanks, Rhonda." Dwayne stapled his resume to his application. Then he submitted his paperwork and returned her stapler.

"Okay, let's see here." She looked his information over. "So, I see that you already have some experience in customer service. And on a cash register as well. How did you like *that*?"

"I liked it a lot. I enjoy meeting people. My register was never short, either. Well, just once, but since it was off by less than a dollar, my manager told me not to worry about it."

"Excellent. And do you have your own transportation?"

"Yes, ma'am."

"Very good. I'll make sure Mr. Carmichael receives this when he comes in this evening, and if he's interested, he'll call you to schedule an interview."

"That sounds great. Thank you so much."

"You're welcome."

Dwayne walked outside, wondering how many places he'd applied to so far that afternoon. He opened his folder and counted how many resumes he had left. "Two," he murmured, calculating that there were now eight businesses in the immediate area who would soon be reviewing his qualifications. And that gave him eight reasons to feel something that he hadn't felt in a very long time: pride.

Dwayne had successfully taken the first step in turning his life around. However, he knew everything wasn't going to become perfect overnight, for a number of hours had passed since he shot up that morning, and his cravings were beginning to come on strong. Fortunately, he had just enough dope to get him through the night, but after that, he'd have to get more.

12

Just before 11 am the following day, Mitch pulled into the gas station on the corner of Trevanion and Montrose, picked Dwayne up, and headed toward the business district. "Dude!" Mitch exclaimed. "I was starting to think... you know, something bad happened to you. Why didn't you take any of my calls yesterday?"

"I was busy."

"Busy? Doing what?"

"Looking for a job."

"A job? You mean like a *real* job? For what?"!

"A lot of reasons. For one thing, I'm sick of having to steal stuff all the time."

Mitch emitted a weird chuckle.

Dwayne looked over at him. "What did you laugh like that for?"

"You dumbass! You're not going to walk right into a job that pays $200 a day!"

"If— I mean, *when* I quit shooting dope, I won't need $200 a day. Even after I get my own place, I shouldn't need much more than $200 for a whole week, as long as I don't spend money frivolously."

"Quit shooting dope? Get your own place? I don't know where you're getting all your cockamamie ideas from, but you better come back to reality, man. There's no way in hell you'll ever quit doing dope. You like it too much. Anyways, it's impossible to quit, so why worry about it."

"It's not impossible. Kathy quit."

"Who?"

"You know. Kathy. Stick's ex-wife."

"No shit, Sherlock! She overdosed. How do you expect her to keep shooting up when she—" Mitch suddenly realized the point Dwayne was making. "Will you just shut up?"!

"No! Look at all our friends who have managed to quit the same way Kathy did—by *dying*! There's Fran, Jimmy, Kim, Charlene, Josh—"

"Shut the fuck up, Dwayne!"

"Greg, Amanda, Zach—"

Mitch slammed on the brakes, leaving two long streaks of rubber on the pavement, until the car came to a rest. "So help me God, Dwayne, if you name one more—"

"Dead, Mitch! Every single one of them! None of them could stop getting high, and now they're all dead! Is that what it's going to take for us to stop! Huh? Is it? What did you say when I got in the car a few minutes ago?"

Mitch wouldn't make eye contact with him, nonetheless answer. He just stared straight ahead as if he was still driving.

"Let me refresh your memory! You said that you were starting to think something bad happened to me. What did you mean by 'something bad,' Mitch? You sure as hell didn't mean you thought I stubbed my toe, now, did you? You were starting to wonder if I overdosed yesterday! Well, no. Not yet, I didn't. Hear me? Not *yet*! Because we're going to, Mitch! We're going to die if we don't quit! And I'm not in the mood to die just yet, are you?"!

Mitch didn't move a muscle or say a word. He just continued staring off into the distance.

Dwayne composed himself and lowered his voice. "I didn't think so. But I know we're not going to quit *today*, so get a move on."

Mitch took his foot off the brake and began accelerating, but he never did reply.

13

"Hurry up in there because I gotta piss," Mitch said, parking in front of a department store.

"I'll see what I can do," Dwayne replied, poking his head back in the window, "but I think 'not getting caught' is a little more important than your urinary requirements."

Carefully following his own rules, Dwayne entered the store, made his selections, and exited with several expensive items.

Seeing him come back outside, Mitch popped the trunk and started the car.

Dwayne jumped back inside and closed his door. Silence ensued once more.

A few miles down the road though, out of the blue, Mitch said, "Next time, I want to be the one who goes in and does the boosting."

"What? No way! What do you know about boosting? You'd get busted for shoplifting in about three seconds! You just mind your business, and keep the getaway car ready."

"You're not my boss! You treat me like I'm nothing but a sidekick, and you've proclaimed yourself 'ringleader,' or something!"

"Ringleader?"! Dwayne turned to him. "Mitch, there's a lot you have to know, to keep from getting caught. It's not as easy as it looks."

"So! You could teach me."

"True. Well, some, I could. But some stuff can't be taught."

"Like what?"

"Like how to keep your composure and remain calm, no matter what happens."

"I can stay cool. I want to be the one who goes inside, and *you* can be the one who waits in the car. My part's boring."

"We'll see, but if I do teach you some of the tricks, I wouldn't wait out in the car. I'd go in and help you, to make sure you don't do anything that would land you in jail."

"That would be okay, I guess."

"Let's just get the stuff we have in the back to Jed for right now, and I'll think about training you down the road. Howard Avenue is coming up. Make a right at the next light."

"I know where he's located."

"Oh, and don't argue with him this time! Thirty-three percent, and we're back out the door, got it?"!

"Me?"!

"Yes, you! Don't provoke him! Just agree with whatever he says, and don't pick a fight with him, even if he is a little, you know, '*off*.'"

"A *little off*? The man's insane, Dwayne! Don't you remember the last time? He saw rain outside and gave you an umbrella for us to use, and it was a beautiful, sunny day!"

"I remember. You just behave."

As soon as Mitch parked the car, Dwayne hustled to the front door, whistled to get Jed's attention, and returned with a smile on his face. "We're good." He hopped back in his seat and shut the door. "Head around back."

Mitch drove down the embankment and made the turn, grimacing as he tried to shift his body into a more comfortable position.

"What the hell's wrong with you?" Dwayne asked.

"I told you I have to piss! It hurts."

"You'll be alright. Maybe Jed will let you use his bathroom."

"I hope so."

Parking behind the store, they exited the vehicle, removed the merchandise from the trunk, and carried it inside.

Mitch hadn't even set the boxes down on the counter yet, when Jed drew first blood. "Well, if it ain't my two most favorite people in the whole world, Dynamite Dwayne and Wonder Puss!"

"Wonder Puss?"! Mitch yelled, stomping over to confront the old man. "I'll 'Wonder Puss' you, you son of a bitch!"

Dwayne jumped between them to prevent a physical altercation. "Let it go, Mitch! Let it go!" he hollered, trying his best not to laugh.

Jed sported the expression of a child flying down the first steep hill of a roller coaster. Relishing in the success of his verbal assault, the wiry, wild-eyed geezer was in such a state of exultation, he could hardly stand still. Smiling from ear to ear, he continued taunting Mitch by making dopey, animated faces at him.

"Quit egging him on, Jed!" Dwayne hollered, struggling to remain between them. "Mitch, go pee! Go find a bathroom somewhere!"

Giving up on trying to get through Dwayne, Mitch stormed off into the cluttered backroom, in search of a bathroom.

"It's located way over there, on the left wall," Jed said, "but you ain't gonna be able to use it."

Mitch stopped in his tracks. "Why not?"!

"Because there ain't no toilet paper in there for you to wipe your girly parts with, when you're done."

"Grrr!" Mitch proceeded to maneuver through the maze of unsold merchandise that Jed had accumulated over the years.

Once he was out of listening distance, Dwayne allowed himself to laugh. "I must admit, Pops, that was funny as shit."

"Uh-huh!" Jed giggled.

"Okay, you've had your fun. Now hurry up and calculate what you owe us before he gets done, so we can just leave when he gets back. Come on, 33%. Start pushing buttons on your adding machine."

Agreeing to his proposal, Jed calculated everything and paid Dwayne—*accurately* this time.

Several minutes passed, and Mitch still had not returned.

"Come on, Mitch!" Dwayne shouted. "Are you lost?"!

"No. I'm almost there." His voice could be heard coming from the middle of the backroom, his body hidden by the clutter.

Soon, he emerged—*grinning*.

Jed studied him. "What's up with you?"

"Me?" Mitch snickered. "Nothing, why?"

"Because of that shitty smile you're wearing. I don't like it. You look like the cat that just ate the canary. What'd you do? You didn't get all caught up in those dirty magazines back there, and choke your chicken in my bathroom, did you?"

"No. I tried to look at one, but I couldn't. The pages were all stuck together."

"Eww!" Dwayne pushed him toward the exit. "Okay, time to leave! See you next time, Jed. Have a good day."

"Yeah! Bye-bye, Jed, ol' buddy!" Mitch laughed on his way out.

"Ol' *buddy*?" Dwayne furrowed his brow and looked at Mitch. "Okay, what did you do?"

"Who, me?" Mitch giggled, getting in the car, wearing an even larger grin. "What makes you think *I* did something?"

"Dammit, Mitch! You're worrying me. Now, what did—"
Just then, Dwayne's cell phone rang. He looked at the incoming number, but he didn't recognize it. "Hello."

Two seconds into the call, his eyes lit up.

The short conversation that followed was composed of limited words, all of which were excitedly spoken.

When he hung up, he looked up in the air, shut his eyes, and yelled, "Woo-hoo!"

"Who in the world was that?" Mitch asked.

"That was Mr. Carmichael! I have a job interview tomorrow at 3 pm!"

14

The shift supervisor popped her head in Mr. Carmichael's office. "Hey Bob, there's a 'Mr. Dwayne Rader' here to see you."

The manager of the grocery store looked up at his cherished pickle-shaped clock (a rare promotional item that a vendor had given him) and smiled. "He's fifteen minutes early. I like him already. Can you show him in, please?"

"Sure." She retrieved Dwayne and escorted him in. "Can I get you something to drink, Mr. Rader. Some water, perhaps?"

"No, thank you."

"How about you, Bob? You need anything?"

"No, I believe I'm all set."

"Okay. Let me know if you change your mind. Do you want me to shut your door on my way out?"

"Yeah, that'd be great. Thanks, Ellen.

Mr. Carmichael took a moment to review Dwayne's application to refresh his memory. Then he picked up his pen and leaned back in his chair. "How are you doing today, Dwayne?" he asked, flipping to his resume.

"I'm well. And you?"

"I'm good. Thanks for asking. So, tell me a little bit about yourself."

"Okay. My name is Dwayne Rader. I'm 22 years old. I'm energetic and outgoing. I enjoy learning new things. And... and I graduated valedictorian in high school."

"Excellent. Those are all very commendable qualities. Did you really graduate at the top of your class?"

"Yes, sir. And I have six college credits as well, in English and physics."

"I see. But how did you acquire those if you never attended college?"

"By passing what's called Advancement Placement Tests, or 'AP Tests,' for short. I took them during my senior year."

"That's quite an accomplishment. And what three words would you say best describe your character traits and personality?"

Dwayne squeezed one eye shut and looked up with the other. "Let's see..." He pondered the question. "Tenacious, sagacious, and nulli secundus."

Mr. Carmichael stopped taking notes. He looked up from his notepad, blinked a couple times, and cleared his throat. "Um, Dwayne?"

"Yes, sir?"

"Are those the kinds of big ten-dollar words that were on your AP Test?"

"That's correct."

"Well, I'm sure glad it was *you* that took that test, and not me, because I'm pretty sure I would have failed the sucker, miserably." He smiled. "I'm not even going to pretend to know what you just said. Can you tell me what those words mean, please?"

"I'm sorry, sir." Dwayne blushed. "I didn't mean to—"

"That's quite alright." Mr. Carmichael raised his hand. "And there is definitely no need to apologize. Be proud of your education. You've neither offended nor embarrassed either of us. I rather welcome the opportunity to learn something new today."

"Whew! Thank you. Tenacious means 'persistent,' in that I never give up, and I always strive to do my best. Sagacious is a term that is used to describe an individual who displays sound judgment. And 'nulli secundus' is Latin for 'second to none,' as in my valedictorian status."

"I must say, I'm impressed."

"Thank you."

Then Mr. Carmichael's expression changed. Dwayne awaited his next question, but the manager remained quiet; he just kept staring at him. After what felt like an eternity, he finally said, "Dwayne, do you mind if I ask you a personal question?"

"No, I don't mind. Ask me anything you like."

"You graduated with a perfect 4.0 GPA. You scored 1530 on your S.A.T. You even have credits toward college classes, and you would most likely be eligible for full scholarships to countless universities. So why on earth did you not go on to college after graduating high school?"

"My father died less than a month after I graduated. Long story short, things got a little crazy after that, and I just never enrolled."

"I understand. I'm sorry about your father's passing. Let's move on to the next question, shall we? Tell me, why do you want to work here?"

"Quite honestly, if you would have asked me that twenty minutes ago, I'm not sure what I would have said. But now, I can say with a great deal of certainty that the main reason I want to work here is because of you, sir."

"Me?" Tilting his head to the side, Mr. Carmichael put his pen down. "Why, *me*?"

"Because I think job satisfaction is determined by *who* a person works for, rather than *where* he works, or the tasks for which he's responsible. People can be in an occupation they love, but still hate their life if they work for someone who disrespects them or treats them poorly. And I find the opposite to be true as well. That being said, I could be assigned the most disgusting job in the world, but still not mind it because of how kind you are, and how nicely I imagine you treat those who are fortunate enough to work for you. Does that make sense?"

"Yes. That makes perfect sense. And thank you for the compliment."

"You're very welcome."

"Well, that's about all the questions I have. What questions do you have for me?"

"How soon are you looking to fill the available positions, and what do they entail?"

"As soon as possible. And the two openings we have are for cashiers, but you wouldn't be stuck on a register the entire time, because we cross-train our associates."

"I like the sound of that."

"Great. Well, given your educational background and professionalism, I'm going to recommend to our district manager that we put you in our management training program from day one. And barring any unforeseen circumstances, I should have some very exciting news for you in the next day or so. Let me run all this by my boss, just as a technicality, and I'll call you in the next 24 to 48 hours."

Dwayne rose to his feet and smiled. "Wonderful!" he said, shaking his hand. "That sounds great. It was a pleasure meeting you, sir, and I look forward to hearing from you."

"The pleasure was all mine, Dwayne. You have a great day, and I'll be in touch with you soon. Bye, now."

"Goodbye, Mr. Carmichael."

15

Unable to get ahold of Mitch, Dwayne walked to the bus stop after his interview, and sat on a knee-high brick wall bordering a flower bed.

He tried calling Mitch again. There was no answer. "Dammit," he muttered, picking a small flower from the nearby garden plot.

Holding its base between his thumb and first finger, Dwayne twirled the velvety-petaled creation around in circles until the stem broke. He watched the flower head fall to the sidewalk, played with the piece that remained in his hand for a little while longer, and then picked another one.

"Impatient!" the elderly woman sitting next to him blurted out.

Dwayne peered up at her. "No. I'm not." Then he looked back down, and recommenced the twirling of his flower.

"Uh-huh." She grinned.

Dwayne paid her no mind, that is, until she insulted him. "Pansy!"

"Excuse me!" Dwayne whirled around to face her. "Did I offend you in some way, ma'am?"!

"No."

"Then why'd you call me a pansy just now. And accuse me of not having any patience a minute ago? Why do you keep pestering me? What's your problem?"!

A large smile fell upon the woman's face. Then she broke into a bit of a snicker and shook her head. "I was referring to the flowers you were picking. The first one was an 'impatiens,' and the kind you're holding now is called a 'pansy.'"

Dwayne closed his eyes and sighed. "I am so sorry for blowing up at you."

"That's quite alright. I guess you could say our conversation was hindered by a 'homophobic hiccup.'"

"Hey, that's funny! You sure–" Just then, Dwayne's phone rang. He snatched it from his pocket and answered it: "It's about time! Where the hell have you been? I've been trying to get ahold of you all afternoon!"

"Dwayne?" a *woman's* voice replied.

A blazing hot, sick feeling ripped through his stomach.

Squeezing his eyes shut, he eased the phone away from his ear. Ever so slowly, he opened his eyes to see if he recognized the incoming number. The screen read, 'Joleen Ramsey.'

Closing his eyes again, he returned the phone to his ear. "Heh-heh-hello." His voice quivered. "Mrs. Ramsey, are you there?"

"Yes. Dwayne? Is that you?"

"Yes, ma'am. I'm sorry. I thought you were a friend of mine calling me back, and I answered my phone without looking at the caller ID. How are you?"

"Other than being stuck in traffic, I'm well. Hey, I know it's short notice, but would you be able to join us for dinner this evening?"

"That would be great, but Mr. Ramsey is using my car today, so I don't have any way to get to your house."

"Oh, that's right. I forgot he borrowed it. Well, where are you right now?

"At the corner of Lincoln and Memorial, waiting on the bus."

Mrs. Ramsey laughed. "I'm only a mile or two away from there. How about if I just pick you up? Would that be alright?"

"Sure, that sounds great."

"Fantastic. I'll be there as soon as I can."

"Okay. Goodbye."

Joleen arrived in a matter of minutes.

"This sure is a nice surprise," Dwayne said, getting in her car.

"Well, that makes *two* of us that are surprised." She gazed at his attire. "I assumed you'd be in jeans, but you look lovely. Why are you wearing a suit?"

"I had a job interview today."

"You did? How did it go?"

"It went great. It's for a cashier position at a grocery store. The manager's already talking about putting me in some kind of fast-track management training program. All he has to do is run it by his boss. He's going to call me in the next 24-48 hours to confirm everything, and then I'll be all set."

"My, heavens, Dwayne, that's wonderful news! I'm so proud of you. What did Jackie say when you told her?"

"Actually, I haven't told her yet. You're the only person I've talked to since I had the interview."

"You told *me* before telling anyone else?" She touched her fingertips to her chest. "My stars, I feel so special."

Dwayne talked about his interview the whole way home, but when Joleen turned into their cul-de-sac, he became distracted by what set in front of the house next door. "Hey, look, Mrs. Ramsey. That's the same kind of car I have, sitting over there."

"Yeah, except that one's yellow, and yours is brown."

"Yeah."

"And speaking of cars, I don't see Clark's. It looks like we beat him home."

Dwayne looked around. "Jackie's car isn't here either. I wonder where she is."

"I don't know," Joleen replied, making her way into the foyer. "They should be here soon. I have a lot to get ready for dinner, anyway."

"Oh, can I help? What are we—"

"Surprise!" Clark and Jackie shouted as they turned on the living room lights, making Dwayne jump out of his skin. "Happy Birthday!"

Dwayne's heart raced. He gasped in disbelief, gaping at all the decorations, streamers, and balloons. "Is all this for me?"

"It sure is!" Jackie gave him a big hug and kiss. "And wait until you see your cake!"

"You bought me a cake too?"

"Nope! Mom and I baked one from scratch."

"You baked one from scratch? I— I don't know what to say. This is amazing. And look at all the balloons and confetti!" He tossed some into the air and smiled.

"I'm so glad you like it," Joleen said. "Now get comfy. Dinner will be ready soon."

"Actually, it's ready *now*." Clark said. "I made it."

"*You* made it? I'm almost afraid to ask, but what, exactly, are we having?"

"Spaghetti with meat sauce." He blew a puff of air on his fingernails and rubbed them back and forth on his chest. "I can make my way around the kitchen okay. I might not be an executive chef, but I'm not entirely helpless."

"Hmmph." Joleen raised her eyebrows.

"Yup!" Jackie said. "And I made the salad and garlic bread."

"Well, I stand corrected. It appears dinner *is* ready."

"Yeah, so let's eat!"

"Are you starving, Clark?"

"No, but the sooner we eat dinner, the sooner we can eat the cake."

"Oh, brother." She turned to Dwayne, sporting a smile. "And after we eat, you get your present."

"My present? You didn't have to get me a present."

"Hush! You just behave, and enjoy being doted on for once. You deserve it."

"Yes, ma'am!" He headed to the dining room, along with everyone else.

16

"Well, I must say, Mr. Ramsey, that was delicious."

"Thank you, Dwayne," Clark replied, adopting a very serious expression. "You know, the recipe for that sauce has been handed down through many generations. The secret is in the complex process of blending the ingredients at just the right time. And even in a specific order. You see, it takes—"

"Pffft! Oh, pah-leeze, Clark!" Joleen looked over at Dwayne. "His secret is that the sauce comes from aisle five of the grocery store, and the only complex process involved was that of the automated machines filling the jars on the company's assembly line."

"Joleen! I think my creative method was—"

"—a bunch of crapola!" She finished his sentence. "Oh! And speaking of the grocery store, Dwayne has some news for all of us, don't you Dwayne?"

"You do? What is it?"

"I had a job interview at the grocery store today."

"You did?"! Jackie exclaimed.

"That's wonderful news, son."

"And they're already talking about putting him in a training program, to groom him for advancement within their organization," Joleen added.

"Holy cow!" Clark leaned back in his chair, placing his hands flat on the table. "Joleen, we could very well be sitting in front of the next CEO of Midway Markets!"

"Whoa!" Dwayne said. "Hold on a minute. First, I have to get a call back from Mr. Carmichael, to confirm I have the job. And secondly, they probably want me to have at least one day's worth of training before they promote me to CEO, don't you think?"

Still leaning back in his chair, Clark's belly bounced up and down as he laughed. "Eh, maybe. But mark my words, you're on the brink of something big. I can feel it in my bones."

Joleen walked over to Clark, held out her finger, and pushed in on his belly.

"Ow!" he grumbled, putting his hand on his stomach. "What the heck's wrong with you?"

"You said you could 'feel it in your bones.' Are you sure you got bones in there? All I feel is a bunch of flab and mush."

Dwayne and Jackie cracked up.

"Ha-ha, very funny. See if I ever toil over a hot stove all day long to make you dinner ever again."

"Toil all day long?"! Joleen took her frustration out on the dish soap, squeezing too much of it in the sink. "Clark, all you did was dump out a jar of sauce and turn on the stove."

"Well!" He huffed, trying to keep a straight face. "Come on, Dwayne. I sense a great deal of tension in the air. Let's you and I retire to the family room." Clark began to walk away. "Wait! Before we leave, I'll get us a couple saucers and forks, and you cut us each another piece of cake to take into the family room, to eat while we watch TV."

"Well, we *could* do that," Dwayne replied, "but that would result in us dirtying two more dishes. Why don't I just grab what's left of the cake, you get two forks, and we'll eat it right out of the pan."

Clark's eyes lit up big and bright. "You got quite a man here, Jackie! Pure genius, he is! You grab the cake, son. And I'll get the forks!"

"Oh, no you don't!" Joleen whirled around, sending soapsuds flying.

"Grab the cake and run, son! Save yourself! Local evil-doers have thwarted the 'fork-portion' of our plan! We'll have to use our fingers! You go that way, I'll go through the game room, and we'll meet at the recliners!"

And just like that, the men disappeared.

Jackie looked over at Joleen. "You know, mom, Daddy can get his 'mush' moving pretty fast when he wants to."

"Uh-huh. Anytime there's something to do with sports, ice cream, or icing, your father can hit around Mach 2."

"Ife Cweam?"! Clark hollered from the family room, with a mouthful of cake. "Did I hear you say you have ice cream to go with this cake?"

"Amazing," Joleen muttered. "He sure doesn't have that kind of hearing when I need him to take the garbage out."

"Can we give Dwayne his present now, mom?"

"Good idea." She turned toward the family room and yelled, "Present-time, Dwayne!"

{Shuffle-shuffle-thump!} "Ouch!" Dwayne yelped, grimacing and holding his knee as he emerged from around the corner.

"Uh-huh! See? That's karma!" Joleen laughed.

"Yeah, I guess so," he groaned, looking around for his gift. "So, where is it?"

"Outside," Clark replied.

"Outside?"

"Yup. Outside."

Everyone walked outside and stood on the front porch. Dwayne looked around. "I don't see anything. Is it hidden?"

"Nope," Clark replied. "Just look around from here. You can't miss it."

Dwayne took on the appearance of a lost puppy.

Jackie couldn't stand it any longer. "Daddy, help him! Give him a hint or something."

"Okay. Here." Clark pulled something out of his pocket and handed it to Dwayne.

"My car keys?"

"That's right."

"My car keys are a hint?" Dwayne scratched his head.

"Yeah. Why don't you go see if they still work."

"Um, because my car's at your garage."

"No, it's not. Your car's right there." Clark pointed to the brightly colored automobile across the way. "And you may want to test the keys in the locks of the doors, to make sure the guy didn't clog any of them up with paint."

"That's *my* car? You had it painted for me?"!

"Do you like it? High-gloss sunshine yellow is a little more cheerful that the color it was before. That brown color looked like shit."

"Clark!" Joleen scolded him.

"Well, it did. His car used to look like a turd with tires."

"Clark!!"

"What? I didn't say 'shit' that time. I said 'turd.'"

"Oh Lord, give me strength." She looked up at the sky.

By this time, Dwayne and Jackie were standing beside the vehicle, admiring its shiny finish.

Clark reached out and held Joleen's hand. They strolled over to Dwayne's car. "Are you sure you like it?"

"Like it? Mr. Ramsey, I *love* it!"

"Get in and start it."

"Why?"

"Just get in and start it."

Doing as Clark requested, Dwayne got in his car, inserted his key into the ignition, and turned it clockwise. "Did it— did it start?" he asked, feeling rather stupid for not being certain.

"Hit the gas and find out," Clark replied.

"VRROOOOM!!"

"Holy shit!" Dwayne yelled. "Whoops! I mean, 'Holy turd!' It sounds brand new!"

"It should. It has a new alternator, starter, battery, spark plugs, plug wires, distributor cap and rotor, filters, brakes, you name it! I think it's got more new parts in it than what it does old, but I wanted you to have something reliable, and it seemed to make for a nice gift, to boot. Happy Birthday, son."

Dwayne walked over to Clark. He stood in front of him for a couple seconds, looking him in the eye. Then he embraced him. "Thanks, dad," he whispered in his ear.

Clark's eyes welled up. "Yeah, well... hu-umm." He cleared his throat, and tried to wipe his eyes without being seen. (Both women saw him, of course. But neither of them ever mentioned it.)

Clark and Joleen walked back inside, leaving the young couple alone.

Jackie strolled over to Dwayne. "I finally have you all to myself," she said, pulling him in close, kissing him passionately. "Happy Birthday, baby."

"Wow, now *that* was a nice birthday kiss. Thank you for my present."

"What present?"

"You know. The car. Getting it all fixed up for me."

"Oh, that's a present from mom and dad. I haven't given you *my* present yet."

"You haven't?"

"Nope."

"Well, when are you going to give it to me?"

"Later."

"Later?" He tilted his head.

"Uh-huh. I rented a hotel room for us. It has a hot tub, room service, and lots of privacy. And I plan on giving you a massage, some kisses, and— come here. Lean down."

Dwayne bent over so she could whisper the rest of her plan in his ear. Then she backed away and said, "Stay here. I just need to go in and tell mom and dad goodbye, and grab my overnight bag. It's already packed, so I won't be long. Okay?"

Dwayne didn't reply. He just stood there, wearing a peculiar expression.

"Dwayne? Are you alright? Why are you so quiet?"

"Because things this good don't happen to regular guys like me. I feel like I'm dreaming, and I don't want to wake up."

"You're not dreaming." She giggled. "And you're not a regular guy. You're *special*. Now stay put, and I'll be back in two shakes of a lamb's tail."

17

"I'm going in," Mitch said, driving into the business district.

"You're what?" Dwayne asked.

"I'm going in."

"You're going into *what*?"!

"The store. I want to experience the thrill of doing the stealing."

"Aw, c'mon Mitch! Don't start that shit again!"

"I'm going in, Dwayne. You can teach me how, and join me. Or you can wait in the car, and wish me luck. You decide."

"You're being ridiculous."

"I'm going in."

"Quit saying that! You're getting on my nerves!"

"Well, I am."

Realizing Mitch wasn't going to give up, Dwayne succumbed to his pressure. "Fine! Listen very closely, okay?"

"Okay." Mitch smiled like an adolescent who'd just gotten his own way.

"Over time, I've come up with seven rules that significantly reduce the risks associated with boosting. Rule number—"

"I know that one of them is to dress up!"

Dwayne looked over at him. "Oh, so *that's* why you wore nice clothes today!"

"Yup, now keep talking. We're getting close. What are the other six rules?"

"Rule number one is, 'don't conceal anything.' In fact, don't even look at any merchandise small enough to be concealed. Rule number two—"

"What's 'concealed' mean?"

"It means, 'able to be stuffed in your pocket.' Now, you already know number two: dress nicely. That means no jeans, shorts, or T-shirts. And *never* any hoodies! Third, don't ever look up at any of the security cameras mounted in the ceiling."

"Why not?"

"Because, dumbass! People who intend to *pay* for stuff never look up at them! The only people worried about where the cameras are, are people who are up to no good."

"Oh."

"Forth, always have a backup plan. Fifth, choose the time you hit the store wisely. You want them to be busy, but not too busy. Right before lunch is best. Most store detectives work the 2 pm–10 pm shift. And never ever steal on weekends. Rule number six, know your security devices. Never attempt to remove any in the store. White rectangular ones are the only ones that will set the alarm off on the way out, so stay away from those. Ink dye packs, spider wraps, and screamers, however, won't set off any alarms, so you can walk right out the doors with those. They're safe to swipe, but don't mess with them in the store or they'll blow up, go off, or do whatever they're designed to do. So don't touch them! And most importantly, rule number seven, no matter what happens, never ever lose your composure or make any rash decisions. Do you have any questions?"

"No, let's go!" Mitch replied, scrambling to get out of the car.

"Wait!"

"What?"

"You're too fired up! Now take a deep breath and calm down! Do you understand everything I just said?"

Mitch took a deep breath. "Yes." He forced himself to reply in solemn manner. "I understand."

"Alright." Dwayne conceded. "Let's go inside."

The two of them exited the vehicle and walked across the parking lot, toward the front of the store.

"Maintain your bearings and sense of direction too," Dwayne added as they made their way through the entrance.

"Uh-huh."

"Are you paying attention to me?"

"Yes. Now stop worrying."

They each grabbed a cart, and proceeded toward the electronics department.

Along the way, Mitch made eye contact with just about everyone. "Dwayne?" he whispered.

"What?"

"The people..." he replied, gawking at two female customers shopping for lingerie. "They're all looking at me. It's giving me the heebie-jeebies."

"They're not looking at you. You're paranoid. Just ignore them. Pretend they don't exist."

Even with the additional advice, Mitch's heart began racing. He was getting a rush, but it wasn't the kind he was expecting. Every cell in his body pulsated with anxiety, his skin glistening with perspiration.

"Here we are," Dwayne said, stooping down in front of the expensive high-definition televisions. "These look nice, don't you think?"

Mitch didn't reply.

Dwayne looked up at him. "I said, 'These look nice, don't you— Dude! Are you okay? You look green!"

Mitch took a deep breath. "Yeah. I'm fine," he replied, wiping sweat from his brow.

"Okay. If you say so. Here, help me load this box. Grab your end and push it up in the air, while I direct my end down inside your cart. It's the only way it's going to fit."

Mitch wiped his clammy palms against his pant legs; grasped the smooth, sheeny box; and lifted it.

"You're going to have to raise it higher than *that*!" Dwayne growled, straining to guide his end in.

"Don't get all pissy! I need to change my grip. Hold still."

"Okay, but whatever you do, don't—"

"OWW! Clang!" The heavy box slipped out of Mitch's sweaty hands, crashed into his face, and fell inside the shopping cart, slamming its metal framework about.

"What the fuck are you doing?"! Dwayne said. "You can't be drawing attention to us like this! Move! Get out of my way so I can put one in my cart—by *myself*!"

Dwayne placed a similar one in his cart, paused, and took a deep breath. "Okay, now follow me up to the front. We'll find a couple unattended registers that aren't roped off, walk between them, and leave out the front door. As for the backup plan, if we're stopped along the way, be friendly: *thank* them for coming to help us, and ask how long it will be until these go on sale. We'll say that we're trying to decide whether to wait until then, or to just go ahead and purchase them today. Understand?"

Mitch appeared attentive, staring off into the distance as he listened. But once again, he didn't reply.

"Mitch, do you understand?"!

"Hey, Dwayne?"

"What?"

"The girl working over by the fitting rooms keeps looking around and texting. She's acting all weird, like she's trying to hide what she's doing from me."

Keeping his hand open and flat, Dwayne smacked Mitch upside his head.

"OWW! Asshole! What was—"

"Shut up, Mitch! I swear to God, allowing your stupid ass to come in here was the worst mistake of my life! The only reason that chick is texting is because she's bored out of her mind. Fitting room attendants aren't allowed to socialize, text, leave their station, or even sit down! She's hiding her phone from her manager, not you, you fucking idiot! Now follow me!"

Overwhelmed by anger and tension, the panic-stricken duo trudged back up to the front of the store.

Feeling like his heart was going to pound out of his chest, Dwayne led Mitch up to the line of registers, located some that were neither manned nor roped off, and walked through them.

With the automatic sliding doors now merely thirty feet away, Mitch became obsessed with their proximity and the patrons up ahead who were closer to freedom than he was.

All he had to do was blend in with the other customers and cruise on out the exit alongside them like nothing was wrong.

But just then, the unthinkable happened: two employees appeared up ahead out of nowhere. They stood side by side, with their arms crossed, barricading the way out.

"Dwayne!" Mitch shrieked in terror.

"Plan B, Mitch," Dwayne replied. "It's okay, just go to—"

"Freeze! Everybody down on the ground!" Mitch hollered, brandishing the 38 caliber revolver that he'd stolen from Jed's junky backroom two days prior, on his way back from the bathroom.

"Mitch! NO!" Dwayne yelled, thrusting his hand up under the weapon, causing it to discharge into a florescent ceiling light.

The ear-splitting gunshot sent customers running in all directions as shattered glass showered floor, and sparks spewed from the ballast.

Paralyzed with fear, Dwayne stood in place as the real-life nightmare unfolded around him.

By the time he snapped out of his incapacitating daze, Mitch had slipped away, and Dwayne was being read his Miranda rights by the police.

18

Cpl. Mayhorn stood behind the thick iron door that housed the inmates in the prison's east wing. Reaching up to his shoulder, he pressed the button on the side of his mike and spoke into it. "Open two fifty, two-five-zero."

The personnel in the control room responded by remotely deactivating the portal's massive lock. Electricity surged into the high-tech device, filling the entire length of the corridor with a God-awful buzzing noise, followed by a loud bang, as a rectangular bolt retracted into the doorway's reinforced steel frame.

Ambling down to the medical holding area, the officer stopped in front of the fourth room. He looked in the one-way mirror at the invalid suffering inside and mumbled, "Damn junkies." Reaching back up to his shoulder, he grabbed his mike again, pressed the button, and gave a second command. "Drop lock on MH-4."

The order initiated another round of abominable buzzing and clanging. "Rader!" Cpl Mayhorn bellowed. "Rader, get up! You got a visitor."

Inside the tiny room, Dwayne lay atop a two-inch-thick, cracked plastic mattress the size of a sleeping bag, shivering.

"Hey!" the officer yelled louder, kicking the metal bunk with his steel-toed boot. "Do you want this visit, or not?"!

"Yeah." Dwayne moaned in agony, as he was being forced to withdraw from heroin cold turkey, in jail.

Using every ounce of energy he had, he stood up, wrapped his sheet around his back and shoulders, and dragged his dead weight down the hall.

"In here, Rader," the corporal said, opening the door to the visiting room.

Lifting his heavy head, he could hardly believe who he saw standing on the opposite side of the smeary plexiglass partition: it was the Ramsey's.

Trembling with fear, Dwayne sat down, picked up the phone, and held it to his ear.

On the other side of the glass, Clark swallowed the lump in his throat, grasped the phone, and held it so that all three of them could hear.

Instead of launching right into questions about what happened, lecturing him, or passing judgment, all Clark said was, "How are you, son?"

Goose bumps blanketed Dwayne's back, and his eyes fell shut, expelling several tears. "I've been better," he replied, wiping his face. "I can't believe you came to see me."

"Don't be silly." Jackie sobbed, forcing a smile. "Why wouldn't we?"

"Be— because I'm a horrible person. And you deserve better than me."

"Dwayne Lawrence Rader, I don't ever want to hear you talk like that again!"

"Jackie's right," Joleen said, "you're not a horrible person."

Jackie pulled the phone closer. "I don't look at us as 'deserving,' or 'not deserving' each other. I just know what I feel in my heart, and we belong *together*. We all make mistakes and flip out sometimes, but when two people have—"

"Yeah, Jackie, but there's more to it than that. I don't know what you've heard, but there's a lot of extenuating circumstances to all of this. In fact, I just need to come clean right now. I have a confession to make. I've kept something a secret from you because I was afraid you'd break up with me if you ever found out. But it's time I face the consequences and tell you anyway." Dwayne hung his head and wept.

"Go ahead, Dwayne, honey. I'm listening."

"Jackie, I'm addicted to heroin. And I'm terrified. It's going to kill me if I don't stop, and I can't stop because I don't know how. I have to steal stuff and then pawn it, to afford my habit. I hate it! I just wanted to get a job, wean myself off the dope, and then live happily ever after with you.

"You know, get a house, maybe a dog, have a couple kids, and come home to you every night, for the rest of my life. That's all I ever wanted and— and now I've ruined it! I've thrown it all away!"

Dwayne started crying so hard, his whole body convulsed.

Jackie whirled around and buried her face in her father's chest, bawling, grabbing fistful after fistful of the back of his shirt.

Clark tried to console her. "Honey, listen." He rubbed her back. "Hold on a minute. Try to stop crying, you two. We haven't got much time. Calm down and listen to me. Dwayne, your attorney will be stopping by later this week to talk to you. I don't want to get your hopes up, but—"

"Mr. Ramsey! I'm sorry for cutting you off, but I don't have an attorney. I'm broke! In fact, I don't even have a public defender yet, nor do I know how—"

"You *have* an attorney, Dwayne. In fact, you have one of the best in the state. I retained him the minute I heard what happened to you, and I already had an emergency meeting with him yesterday to get all the preliminary stuff out of the way. That way, you two can get right down to business when he gets here, okay?"

Dwayne and Jackie looked stunned. As did Joleen.

"Oh, Daddy!" Jackie burst into tears, squeezing him tightly.

"Now princess, like I said, we can't get our hopes up, but all is not lost—not by a long shot. Okay, your mother and I are going to step outside so you two can spend your last minute or two speaking privately, but Dwayne, you keep your chin up. Just hang in there, and we'll see what tomorrow brings... *Dr. Wicked's* orders." He winked at him on his way out.

"Mr. Ramsey?" Dwayne called to him.

"Yes, Dwayne?"

"I just wanted to say 'thank you.' No matter what happens, I sincerely appreciate everything you've done for me. I— I'm honored to be part of your family, and I promise that my actions will show it, if I ever get a chance to prove myself."

"I put money on a phone account here so you can call us, too. Say your prayers, get some sleep, meet with your attorney, and keep in touch. Your trial's going to be here before you know it, and we have a lot to get done before then. Bye, son."

"Bye, dad."

19

"All rise." The bailiff instructed everyone in the room to stand. "Court is now in session with the Honorable Judge Wicklander presiding."

The distinguished magistrate emerged from his chambers, ascended the steps to the platform, and peered out at the attendees. "Be seated," he said in a commanding tone of voice, taking his place on the bench.

"The next case on the docket is, 'The State of Maryland versus Dwayne Rader,'" the state's attorney announced. "Mr. Rader is being charged with malicious mischief, reckless endangerment, disorderly conduct, assault in the first degree, assault in the second degree, possession of a firearm, possession of CDS-not marijuana, robbery, and armed robbery, your Honor."

"And how does the defendant plead?"

"Guilty, your Honor," Dwayne's attorney, Mr. Ralph Shipley, replied.

"You may proceed with your client, counselor."

Mr. Shipley began speaking very rapidly to get the routine preface out of the way. "Mr. Rader, you have chosen to enter a plea of 'guilty.' In doing so, you have elected to forfeit your right to a jury trial, and all the benefits that are traditionally associated with having a jury. You have also entered this plea knowingly, intelligently, and voluntarily in that you have not been bribed, threatened, coerced by anyone or promised anything. If everything I have said is true, please signify by saying so at this time."

In the few seconds it took Mr. Shipley to rush through his spiel, Dwayne's life flashed before his eyes. He watched his attorney's mouth move a thousand miles an hour but heard absolutely nothing. It was as if he had gone deaf.

During the period of silence, his mind took a peaceful, picturesque journey into his past, where he reminisced about fond childhood memories: he saw himself excitedly unwrapping presents on Christmas morning, and wearing his comfy, one-piece pajamas that zipped up the front. He saw his dad taking him out in the ocean on vacations to the beach, holding him tight in his arms as big waves came in and splashed into them. Memories of blowing out birthday candles, visiting his grandparents, and going to carnivals flowed through his mind like a serene river in the country. Every episode was filled with innocent giggles and elated squeals. He recalled adoring bedtimes, for when he was small, his dad used to cradle him snugly and swing him, hollering, "One for the money, two for the show, three to get ready, and four to *go!*" And on "go," he'd throw him onto the bed, where he'd bounce and laugh. And then he'd position all of his stuffed animals perfectly, making sure they could all see over the top of each other and breathe okay.

The last memory he had was of his mother tucking him in, kissing him, and softly saying, "Goodnight, Dwayne... Dwayne... Dwayne!!" his attorney was yelling loudly and repetitively, trying to snap him out of his state of unresponsiveness.

"Huh?"

"Well?"! Mr. Shipley said.

Dwayne's heart raced, sweat pouring from his body. He blinked a couple times and asked, "Well, *what*?"

Mr. Shipley leaned in close to him and whispered, "Say out loud that you agree with what I just said."

"Uh, yeah. I agree," Dwayne mumbled.

The judge peered down at him. "Hmmm," he said, tapping his chin. "Dwayne Rader. Didn't you appear before me a few years ago?"

"Yes, your Honor."

"And what was the outcome of that trial?"

"You sentenced me to nine years, all suspended but six months, with two years of probation."

"I see. And has that probationary period expired?" Judge Wicklander inquired, intentionally asking edgy questions to which he knew the answers, solely to torment the young recidivist.

"No, sir. I still had two months remaining when this incident occurred."

"So... you commit a string of burglaries two years ago. I make you spend only six months in jail. And *knowing* you have over eight years worth of backup time still hanging over your head, you get arrested *again*?"! He scrutinized Dwayne's list of new charges. "The two robbery and two assault charges, alone, carry— let's see... 15, 20, 25, and 10 —carry a maximum penalty of seventy years in prison, Mr. Rader, and that's not including the eight years for violating your probation, *or* any time for your current, lesser charges!"

Dwayne closed his eyes, his body trembling.

Leaving him to his own devices, Judge Wicklander then turned his attention back to the prosecuting attorney. "What's the state's recommendation in this matter?"

"The state is willing to drop all charges except for the one count of armed robbery. We do, however, ask that the court sentence Mr. Rader to the maximum twenty years for that count. We also ask that Mr. Rader serve the balance of eight-and-a-half years in the form of a consecutive sentence for the violation of probation, your Honor."

"Uh-huh..." the judge murmured, rubbing his cheek as he pondered the state's proposal. "Do you have anything else?"

"No, your Honor. The state has nothing further."

Judge Wicklander looked at Dwayne's attorney. "Counselor, what would you like to add, before I render my verdict?"

"Your Honor, Mr. Rader is only twenty-three years old. He graduated at the top of his class in high school. Not twentieth, and not even second or third. He was the valedictorian, graduating with a perfect 4.0 GPA in a class of 357 individuals. Additionally, Mr. Rader possesses an unprecedented level of ethicality, politeness, and professionalism. He is, your Honor, the epitome of a perfect gentleman.

"After his father passed away, however, Mr. Rader's life crashed down around him. And shortly thereafter, he made one fatal decision: he began using drugs to dull the pain of losing his dad. And I say '*fatal*,' not because heroin has killed Mr. Rader," Mr. Shipley said, turning to Dwayne. "It just hasn't killed him *yet*!

"And I say 'yet,' because that's the truth, your Honor. It *will* kill him. It's only a matter of time." Mr. Shipley made his way to the front of the courtroom, where he swaggered about with an unparalleled aura of confidence. "In fact, it's been scientifically proven that people have a greater chance of recovering from *cancer*, than what they do recovering from drug addiction. Furthermore, drug addiction, just like cancer, is categorized as a 'disease' by the American Medical Association."

Mr. Shipley stopped walking. "It's true. The AMA classified drug addiction and alcoholism as diseases back in 1966. So, think about my earlier comment for a minute and truly digest it: someone living with the disease of cancer has a better chance of surviving-" He made deliberate eye contact with the judge. "-than what someone living with the disease of addiction does. And it is my contention, your Honor, that the state has failed to take any of this into consideration, prior to making their recommendation.

"When the state looks at Mr. Rader, all they see is a common criminal. A thief. A vagabond. A scoundrel. But do you know what I see when I look at Mr. Rader? I see a man who can speak two languages! I see a man with potential! I see a future business leader!" Mr. Shipley became louder with each proclamation, thrusting his pointer finger higher into the air each time he said "I."

Then he became quiet, trudged back to the table with Dwayne, and sighed. "But I also see a very sick man," he said in a heartfelt, emotional manner. "I see a man with a disease. And I see a man who's in grave danger of breathing his last breath if he doesn't get help.

"Days before his arrest, your Honor, Mr. Rader took it upon himself to apply for various jobs in the area. And not only did he get an interview, he actually landed a job—a job which he was to begin the Monday following his arrest.

"His plan was to become employed, become a productive member of society, and tackle his disease by himself. And that, your Honor, shows an incredible desire to stop using drugs.

"Furthermore, not only does it depict an unprecedented level of initiative and determination, it *proves* that he was actually in the process of executing his action plan, in a dire attempt to turn his life around on his own. To utilize an old cliché, Mr. Rader was not just 'talking the talk,' he was indisputably 'walking the walk.' And that's highly commendable in my eyes, your Honor.

"As you deliberate on whether or not to imprison this young man for the next three decades, I respectfully request that you take into consideration all that I have brought to light, from his high level of intellect and positive upbringing, to his genuine desire for a better way of life.

"At this time, I would like to submit to the court for review, Mr. Rader's high school transcript depicting his 4.0 GPA and valedictorian status, the offer letter he received from the grocery store regarding the job he managed to secure just prior to his arrest, and lastly, literature and an acceptance letter from ARCS, which I will explain momentarily."

Judge Wicklander nodded to the bailiff, instructing him to retrieve the documents from Mr. Shipley. "In the interest of time, counselor, verbally summarize what you're giving me that pertains to ARCS. What's ARCS?"

"Certainly, your Honor. ARCS stands for Arizona Recovery Center for Survival. It's an intense, inpatient drug rehabilitation program that not only teaches individuals how to successfully abstain from drugs, it teaches them how to survive living in the desert. Operationally, it's—"

"Excuse me, counselor. Did you say, 'in the *desert*'?"

"Yes, your Honor, that's correct. The addicts who enroll in this program are transported to barren land in the southwest, where they learn how to live on a day-to-day basis without drugs. The premise is this: if they can survive and learn how to live without drugs in an extremely harsh environment, and under an unspeakable amount of stress, then they should experience minimal difficulty continuing to live a drug-free life when they reenter society—a place where there exists luxuries like running water, electricity, and temperatures under 115 degrees."

The judge sat upright in his chair and put on his reading glasses. "There's a warning printed on the back of this one pamphlet that says each participant is responsible for carrying his own antivenin."

"That's true. It's a very unorthodox approach, to say the least. Their staff of specialists is also extraordinary in that, besides being highly qualified, they conduct themselves like drill sergeants. The overall environment is that of an old-school military camp.

"That being said, I took the liberty of having Mr. Rader evaluated by the Health Department, and they determined that he qualifies for an 8-505. My intuition led me to believe that your Honor would most likely reject a request for an 8-505, if I merely suggested it in conjunction with one of our local facilities, so I researched the matter until I located this one in Arizona.

"Given its unique attributes—and the benefits I'm certain Mr. Rader would reap from the program—I humbly request that your Honor approve my client for an 8-505 to ARCS."

Judge Wicklander read the literature for a little while longer. Then he put everything down and glared at Dwayne. "I think what I'm going to do is—" He began to divulge his ruling but then unexpectedly paused, nearly crippling Dwayne at the knees. "Counselor, may I see the results of Mr. Rader's Health Department evaluation?"

"Certainly." Mr. Shipley handed the report to the bailiff.

After reviewing it, the judge rested his forearms atop his desk, interlocked his fingers, and looked right at Dwayne. "Mr. Rader, do you fully understand what an 8-505 is, and what it would require of you if I did, in fact, entertain this request?"

Dwayne felt his mouth open but no words came out. Paralyzed with fear, he was incapable of speaking.

Unsatisfied with his inaudible response, the judge elected to explain it. "If I grant you an 8-505, it means that you would go to this rehabilitation program in lieu of going to jail; and there, you would be taught how to overcome your drug addiction. You'd stay there for nine months. And if you successfully complete the program, you'd get to return to Maryland as a rehabilitated man, and be granted a fresh start.

"But, if you fail to complete the program for any reason, you'll go to prison for this new charge, and also for violating probation. This would be the final chance you'd ever have at living a normal life, Mr. Rader.

"I have to tell you though, what I am inclined to do, is to just send you to prison where you would have a good chance of being sexually assaulted. You would have a good chance of being stabbed. You would not do well there, Mr. Rader. I'm just not sure if I should give you this last opportunity, or not. Part of me thinks I would just be wasting a lot of peoples' time and accomplish nothing more than delaying your inevitable incarceration."

Dwayne couldn't do anything but stand there. Sweating profusely, he remained silent and motionless. The mental anguish was unbearable, for the next three decades of his life was about to be decided upon in the next three seconds.

Finally, Judge Wicklander reached for his gavel, cleared his throat, and handed down his decision: "In the case of Maryland versus Dwayne Rader, I find the defendant guilty of one count of armed robbery, and I am imposing a sentence of twenty years. And regarding the violation of probation, I am imposing an additional eight years, in the form of a consecutive sentence."

When Dwayne heard that he had been sentenced to 28 years in prison, his vision blackened and his right knee buckled. He was about to pass out.

Then Judge Wicklander finished his thought: "I am also granting the defendant an 8-505—to be completed at the ARCS facility in Arizona—thereby suspending the 28 years, pending Mr. Rader's successful completion of the aforementioned program.

"However, should Mr. Rader fail to complete the ARCS program, he is to be immediately extradited back to Maryland, where he will serve his sentence at the Division of Corrections in Jessup, MD.

"We'll take a ten minute recess." Judge Wicklander struck the desk with his gavel.

20

Clark, Joleen, and Jackie were the first visitors to show up at the jail the following day, arriving forty-five minutes before visiting hours even began.

"Look, here he comes!" Jackie hollered, watching Dwayne emerge from the rear corridor with four other inmates.

Wearing a humongous smile, Dwayne took a seat in the closest booth and picked up the phone.

On the other side of the plexiglass, Jackie clutched the receiver. "Hi, honey! How are you?"

"I'm doing great, now that yesterday is over."

"Jackie, hold the phone away from your ear some, so we can all talk to him at the same time," Clark said, turning his attention to Dwayne. "You did a great job yesterday, son."

"Me? Uh-huh. If you're talking about sweating, stammering, and nearly soiling myself, yeah, I did wonderfully. The only reason I'm not spending the next thirty years in prison is because of you, Mr. Ramsey. If you wouldn't have hired Mr. Shipley to represent me, I would have been judicially slaughtered. You saved my life, sir."

"Aw, Dwayne, I didn't—"

"Yes. You did. And I won't ever forget it. I'm going to make you all proud of me, I promise."

"Dwayne, we *are* proud of you," Joleen said.

"Yes, very proud," Jackie added.

"Thanks, honey. You really are something else! I love you so much."

"I love you too, dear. And Dwayne?"

"Yeah?"

"Were you being serious about us having a house with a picket fence, a dog, and a couple kids someday? Or were you just talking about those kinds of things because you were so upset?"

"Jackie, as God as my witness, I have never been more serious about anything in my life. I don't *ever* want to be without you, and after I get back from Arizona, I won't ever have to be."

Jackie's eyes welled up. "You're so sweet." She put her hand flat against the glass.

On the opposite side, Dwayne put his hand directly opposite hers, finger-for-finger, and smiled.

"Huh-umm." Clark cleared his throat, for even he, despite his tough guy image, was becoming choked up. "Alright, you two... Cut it out before you make *me* cry."

Jackie and Dwayne chuckled. "Oh my, it feels so good to have yesterday over with." Dwayne chortled. "For a while there, I didn't think I was ever going to see the light of day again, nonetheless laugh.

"I was blown away when Mr. Shipley presented my transcripts and job offer letter to the judge. I wonder how he got all that stuff."

"I gave everything to him," Clark replied.

"Really? How did *you* get them?"

"I took the liberty of asking your mother for them. I hope you're not mad."

"Mad? Don't be ridiculous, sir. I could never get upset with you. Anytime you think something is a good idea regarding my well-being, just do it. I trust you. By the way, how was mom when you saw her?"

Clark swallowed hard. "Um..." He looked down at the ground. "Well..."

"That's okay, Mr. Ramsey. You don't have to say anything. I'm sorry you had to go there and see her like that. I'm surprised she was able to find my transcripts."

"They were in your room. And your letter from the grocery store was lying on the kitchen table. We told her what happened to you, but I don't know if she'll remember us being there. May we check in on her from time to time while you're away?"

"You'd do that for me?" Dwayne's eyes lit up.

"Sure."

"Yes, I'd really appreciate that. And I swear, one day I'm going to kill that Barry for enabling her like he does!"

"Now, you just focus on your *own* recovery right now," Clark said. "We'll look after your mother while you're gone. And don't worry about Barry. These things have a way of working themselves out. You know what I mean, Dwayne?" He winked at him.

"One minute remaining!" the officer yelled. "Start wrapping it up."

"Hey, they said I only have a minute left!" Dwayne started talking really fast. "Listen, I love you all, and I'll see you when I get back! Oh, and Mr. Shipley said we're not allowed to have cell phones at ARCS. And there aren't post offices out there either, so I doubt if we'll hear from each other for a while.

"Anyway, thanks for everything! And if it's not a problem, could you keep an eye on my car for me, since you did all that work to it?"

"Don't you worry about a thing," Clark said. "I already locked it in my garage. And to ensure my future son-in-law's safety, by the time you return, we'll have the spare room in our house fixed up for you to use as a bedroom. I prefer you live with us after you complete your recovery program, until you and Jackie can afford a place of your own. Okay?"

Dwayne's mouth dropped open, and his eyes got as big as saucers. "Can I really live with you guys? And share holidays with you? And come home every evening to tell you how my day was at work? And eat Mrs. Ramsey's incredible cooking all the time?"!

"Oh, Dwayne!" Joleen giggled. "You're too much!"

"Yes." Clark smirked. "It'll all be ready for you by the time you come home. To your *new* home. Our home."

"Okay, Rader! Time's up!" the officer hollered.

"I have to go now. Thanks again for everything. I love you, Jackie."

"I love you too, honey! Be safe! I'll miss you."

"I'll miss you, too. I can hardly wait to come back, so we can begin 'living happily ever after' with each other."

"Me too." She blew him a kiss.

21

Under the blistering midday sun, Dwayne sat handcuffed and shackled inside the hot metal bed of a pickup. He was being hauled out to the desert.

Excluding the felons with whom he was sharing his ride, it had been thirty minutes since he'd seen another human being.

With his back against the cab of the truck and his legs outstretched, he watched the dust kick up behind them as they thundered across the roadless, bone-dry earth, leaving behind a brown contrail that neither drifted nor dissipated in the desiccated air.

As far as the eye could see, in every possible direction, there existed a flawless linear horizon where the sky met the sand. Dwayne gazed at it.

Just as he began to relax, he felt the truck slow down, and heard someone yell something about where to park.

The driver made a slight right, drove past a huge pit, and came to a stop between two large tents.

Up ahead, there were some smaller tents, a few vehicles, and something that resembled an irrigation truck.

"Good afternoon, ladies!" a man wearing loose white clothing said, twirling his billy club from its leather strap as he approached.

The driver gave him a smile. "Hot 'nuf for ya, Rob?" he asked, climbing out of the cab of his truck.

"Aw, it ain't bad. I don't even think it's supposed to hit 100 today. You should've been here a few days ago, when it hit 118. Now *that* was toasty."

"Screw that!" Albert shoved his finger in his mouth, into the crevice behind his lower lip, and removed an enormous wad of chewing tobacco. "Come on, boys." He opened the tailgate. "Scooch on down here thissah way, so I can get them cuffs off ya."

Using their legs to scoot along like inchworms, the three passengers made their way to the back of the truck.

"So, what do we have, here? They look a little scrawny, if you ask me. And what's the deal with him on the end?" Rob nodded to the man wearing an eyepatch.

"Beats me. I just cuff 'em, load 'em, and bring 'em out here to you like I'm told."

Rob strutted down to the individual in question. "Well! What's your story, Cyclops? You got a birth defect or something?"!

"No. When I was cleaning my bong out with rock salt and rubbing alcohol a few years back, I blew into it, causing the shit inside to spray back in my face."

"And it blinded you?"

"Yup."

"Well, you know what they say: 'it's all good fun until someone loses an eye.' You're not real bright, are you boy? So, why are you here?"

"Because my parents scored me a kick-ass attorney who convinced the judge to send me to a nine month rehab, instead of shipping my ass off to prison."

"No, shit-for-brains! What crime did you commit to be facing prison time? So far, the only things I can see you're guilty of is being stupid and having a smart mouth, neither of which are jailable offenses. You didn't get here for pick-pocketing Pa Kettle to buy yourself a little wacky weed, now, did ya, boy?"!

"No! I stabbed a guy in the gut for not giving me his wallet when I told him to. I'm a dope fiend, dickhead!"

"Dickhead, huh? I see," Rob murmured, smacking his baton into his opposite hand as he approached the man in the middle. "What's your name?"

"James, sir."

"And what's your story?"

"I've been addicted to crack for years. I've lost everything: my business, my wife, my money, my house. Everything. It's all gone."

"Yeah? And...?"!

"And I don't want to go to prison. And I don't want to keep getting high. I begged the judge to give me this opportunity because I want to make something of my life, you know, while there's still time."

Remaining motionless, Rob stared into the individual's eyes for a moment. Then he looked over at Dwayne. "And how about you, pretty boy?"

"I don't want to get high anymore, either. All my friends are dead. They all overdosed. And I don't want to die. I'm sick of having to steal stuff all the time, to afford my habit. I once had a good life, sir. But now my life sucks! Well, except for my girlfriend and her parents. They support me. But anyway, once I get well, then I want to get my mom some help, too."

"Is she a heroin addict?"

"No, she's hooked on pills."

"I see." He took a step back. "Okay, all three of you turn around and place your hands behind your back."

Given that they'd only been uncuffed for three minutes, the request didn't make much sense. Regardless, James and Dwayne did as they were told. But the man on the end did not. "Why?"! He demanded to know.

"Because I said so, Cyclops!"

Reluctantly, the one-eyed man turned around and put his hands behind his back. Without Rob having to say anything, Albert handcuffed and shackled him.

Figuring they were next, James and Dwayne waited to be restrained, but Albert backed away.

"Okay, men." Rob said. "Turn around and face me."

"Hey! Why the fuck didn't you handcuff *them?* Why just me? What's going on?"!

"I'll tell you what's going on, Cyclops! The two men to your right are appreciative of this opportunity. They genuinely want a better life. They want to learn how to abstain from drugs. Furthermore, they are respectful and obedient.

"You, however, possess absolutely none of these attributes! You have no desire, whatsoever, to stay clean. I know 'your kind,' Cyclops! You planned on just going through the motions of completing this program in order to stay out of jail, and you would have gotten high as soon as you returned home—probably within hours of graduating. You would have gone right back to your old ways of robbing, stealing, and using; and I refuse to waste my time with a hopeless loser like you."

"What do you mean, I *would have* graduated? And why am I in handcuffs?"!

"This program is not for you," Rob replied. "You have just failed. You will—"

"Failed? I just fucking got here! You can't fail me! I got twenty years backup! My dad's the CEO of Kleb International! What do you want? He'll pay you whatever you want to pass me! I can't go to prison for twenty years!"

"You can, and you will. Now get your ass back up in the bed of that truck."

The one-eyed man stared into Rob's eyes for a second. Then he spit in his face.

Rob wiped the grotesque glob of phlegm from his cheek. Then he retrieved a teeny black canister from his pants pocket, and shot the man in his one good eye with a stream of pepper spray.

"Ahhh!!" The guy screamed, his body collapsing to the ground.

Reaching down, Rob and Albert "encouraged" him to stand back up and slide into the bed of the truck by pulling his ears upward, and twisting, causing him to wail as he rose to his feet.

"There ya go!" Albert laughed. "Good boy. Hey Rob, lock him onto that-there eyehook, up by the cab, so he don't go floppin' outta my truck on the way back, will ya?"

"Sure. I got him." Rob secured the troublemaker.

"Thank ya, kindly." Albert nodded to him. "Welp, I gotta run. Me and the wife are gonna hit the pig roast over at the fire hall tonight fer dinner, and I don't wanna get late. I'll see ya next time. Take 'er easy now, ya hear."

"You do the same." He waved.

"Right-O!" Albert climbed up into the cab of his truck.

"Alright, you two!" Rob gestured toward the largest tent. "March! Get in there so we can go over the rules, issue you your uniforms, and get this show on the road! The door to your left! Go!"

22

"Go over to the far wall, grab a box, and bring it back here," Sgt. Courtney said. "We're going to make sure you have all your intake supplies before you sign for them."

James and Dwayne each retrieved a box.

"First, take out your uniforms. You should have three black-and-white striped shirts, three matching pants, four towels, four pairs of white socks, four pairs of pink underwear, and we'll get you sized for shoes in a moment. Count carefully. Use your toes if you have to! Are you good, so far?"

Dwayne held up a pair of his underwear, pinching them as if they *already* contained fecal matter. "Pink?" he muttered. "Rob, why are—"

"Stop right there! Don't ever address me by my first name as if we are equals! It's disrespectful. I am your superior! You will do as I say. You will not question my authority. You will address me as 'sergeant,' 'sir,' or 'Sgt. Courtney.' Never 'Rob.' Do I make myself clear?"!

"Yes, sir. I apologize. I didn't mean to offend you."

"Apology accepted. Next, you should have a bar of soap, a toothbrush, a wash cloth, a bath towel, deodorant, shampoo, a can opener, two plates, two bowls, two cups, a Big Book from Alcoholics Anonymous, two antivenin kits, a Bible, and an ARCS handbook. So far, so good?"

Rummaging through their boxes as fast as they could, they counted most of what Sgt. Courtney had rattled off, and assumed the rest was there.

"Yes, sir."

"Excellent! Now have a seat, and we'll hit some of the highlights in your handbook. You're responsible for complying with all of it though, not just the highlights, so I strongly recommend you have all of it read by tomorrow night.

"The first few pages contain your schedule. We get up every morning at 6 am. Throughout the day, you'll see blocks of time designated for eating, classroom sessions, personal time, field work, etc. Personal time is to be prioritized. Personal hygiene, laundry, and chores come before activities like playing cards, watching television, and the like."

"Television?" James said. "Excuse me, sir, but how do we watch television with there being no electricity out here?"

"We have a TV. It's hooked up to a machine next to a stationary bike. If you want to watch it, you have to get on the bike and pedal. Pedaling produces electricity which, in turn, supplies power to the television set. Channels are limited, but it's better than nothing."

"Suppose two guys want to watch TV at the same time?"

Sgt. Courtney laughed. "I don't think you'll ever have to worry about that. It's rarely used as it is. Participants in this program are typically far too tired to pedal a bike after they complete their daily field work."

"What do you mean by, 'field work,' sir?"

"Coal mining," the sergeant replied.

James and Dwayne looked at each other. "Coal mining?"

"That's right. The southwest is very rich in mineral resources. We're not only going to teach you how to abstain from using drugs, we're going to teach you the value of a dollar.

"Moreover, we're going to show you that you're capable of making money via legitimate means. No longer will you have to steal things like you're used to doing.

"We're going to teach you how to work hard, feel good about yourself, budget your money, and lead a life you can be proud of.

"We're going to read the Bible together, cover to cover, studying and discussing ten pages per day. The version we use is called 'The Life Recovery Bible.' It's 1,670 pages long. Reading ten pages per day, James, how many days will it take us to read and fully understand the Bible, in its entirety?"

"Um... 167?"

Sgt. Courtney sighed. "Are you asking me, or are you telling me?"

"I'm telling you."

"You are? You sound pretty damn uncertain to me! Are you sure?"!

"Yeah."

"Then tell me like you're sure!"

"167."

"167, what?"

"167, sir."

"I can't hear you!"

"167 days, sir!" James belted out.

Sgt. Courtney leaned back in his chair and smiled at the young man. "There you go," he said in a soft, sincere tone of voice. "Maybe I forgot to mention, we teach confidence here, too. That felt good, didn't it?"

James smiled. "Yes, sir. It did."

"Confidence. Pride. Being a leader, not a follower. Being a good role model. Speaking with authority, yet remaining grateful and humble. By the time you leave here, you will have mastered such qualities, and in doing so, you will possess the ability to ascertain anything you want in life, as long as you never go back to doing drugs. Do you understand?"

"Yes, sir."

"Good. Now, to return to your question, I— I, uh..." The sergeant paused and scratched his head. "Shit! Now I forgot what your original question was! What did you ask me again?"

"I asked you what 'field work' was, and you said it referred to coal mining, but I—"

"That's right! Yeah, the southwest is full of coal. Big underground pockets contain billions of tons of the stuff, but locating it can be very difficult. That's where you all come in. Between your classroom sessions and personal time, we put you to work.

"Before each shift, you will be issued a pickax. You'll use it to dig for coal. And then at the end of each shift, I'll collect them before you leave to go shower, eat, or whatever. Most men opt to shower after bustin' their ass for ninety minutes in 110 degree heat.

"Makeshift showers stick out of the water truck out back. Get under one, pull the chain, and you're in business. You get paid five dollars a day. Cans of food like pears, tuna, green beans, and spaghetti cost between a quarter and fifty cents. Powdered milk, good-smellin' soap, disposable razors, toothpaste, and all that jazz are ten to twenty cents. Most guys save a couple bucks out of their pay to gamble for entertainment at night, and that's fine. But there's to be no fighting, no stealing, and no being loud after 9 pm. No cell phones, no mail, and no disobeying orders. No lousy attitudes, no bullshit, and no beatin' off in plain view of other men. Do you chores, do your classroom homework, and follow all the rules. Show officers and instructors respect, and you'll receive it. Show the other participants respect, and you'll *probably* receive it—some guys are a little rough around the edges yet, but their desire to get clean is strong, so we're giving them a chance. And the ones coming off crystal meth are downright cuckoo in the head, but their nutty behavior and delirium will subside as time progresses. In the meantime, keep in mind that they're paranoid individuals who may very well be hallucinating when they look at you, so be extra careful when they're working near you with a pickax. Any questions so far?"

"Yes, sir." Dwayne spoke up. "I noticed that our uniform shirts are long sleeve. Given how hot it is out here, why aren't we permitted to have short sleeve shirts? And why are our towels in with our uniforms, and not with our bathroom supplies?"

"Good questions. The answer is that you need to keep your skin covered with a thin fabric, or you'll fry to a crisp. Always minimize your skin's exposure to the sun.

"Regarding the towels, soak one in cool water and put it on your head at the start of each shift. It'll keep you cooler, longer. Some days, you'll work only one shift. Other days, you'll work two or three, but never more than three."

"Sergeant Courtney?"

"Yes, James?"

"What happens when we find coal? Are we supposed to dig out the billions of tons all by ourselves?"

"No. We dig pits about the size of the one you saw out there on your way here. If we find coal, all we do is contact the authorities, and the government will bring in their own crews and strip-mining equipment to extract it.

"And if we *don't* find any—which happens a lot—we just move on to a different spot and start digging another hole. Sometimes we move five miles away. Sometimes we move twenty-five miles away. We can go in any direction we want. You'll see what I mean real soon. We're actually moving to a new location in the next day or two."

"Really?"

"Yes. Everyone has assigned tasks on moving day, and as soon as the man in charge of taking a head count gives us the green light, we hit the road! Well, that would be the proper expression if roads existed out here, but you get my drift."

"Has anyone ever tried to escape?" James asked. "It just seems odd to me, because there aren't any bars or chains keeping us here."

"Oh, sure. A few people have over the years."

"They have? Did anyone ever find them? What did the escapees do? I bet they moved to another country!"

"Nope," the sergeant replied. "Nothing of the sort. You have to remember, we're over ten miles from even the smallest of towns out here, at any given time. The only thing that running away does, is initiate one of the slowest, most agonizing suicide trips known to man. Daytime temperatures out here can exceed 120 degrees, and at night, it often drops below freezing. Imagine—"

"Below freezing?"!

"Yes, but in remains relatively warm in the tents. Besides that, there are plenty of blankets to cover up with, if you get chilly. Some people decided to brave the frigid cold though, and take off during the night. Others opted for a daytime departure. But regardless of when they chose to run away, they all died. Most of 'em literally cooked to death like you would imagine, but some also perished in the middle of the night."

"How?" Dwayne asked. "People don't freeze to death just because it just gets down to thirty degrees for a few hours."

"No, but when it drops below sixty, it becomes impossible for anyone to hide from the animals who come out at night to hunt. Nocturnal predators use thermal imaging to find food, and a human being's body temperature is 98.6 degrees; a raging bull in a china shop would stand out less than a person walking through the desert, after dark! Escapees are stalked, attacked, and killed. End of story. Hell, sometimes the ordeal doesn't even entail the 'stalking' part, like when the one guy fell into a nest of fire ants. And another time, a man was bitten by a rattler. But that doesn't count."

"Doesn't count?"! Dwayne exclaimed. "Why doesn't the snakebite victim count?"!

"Because he wasn't bitten once, he was bitten multiple times. Not only that, but he had his antivenin with him and chose not to use it. That being known, it can be safely assumed that he intentionally provoked the snake to repetitively bite him."

"Now why in the hell would he have done that?"!

"Because he'd been on the run in the desert for 36 hours. Half way into his trip, I guarantee he was dehydrated so bad that all his major muscle groups were drawn into permanent, painful cramps, rendering him immobile. I can't even imagine the kind of physical and psychological agony he must have underwent, wondering how long he'd have to lie there until his organs finally shut down. Trust me, to him, that snake was heaven-sent. Fortunately, he was able to grab ahold of it good 'nuf that it couldn't get away. See, the longer he managed to hold onto it, the more times it bit him; and the more times it bit him, the quicker he knew he would die, and not have to suffer any longer."

James and Dwayne both looked horrified; a short period of silence ensued.

"Well!" Sgt. Courtney suddenly hollered, smacking his palms down onto his thighs, making the pair of them jump. "Let's get you two fitted for shoes, and then I'll take you over to your quarters and introduce you to the guys."

23

"Everyone's on their afternoon break right now," Sgt. Courtney said, escorting James and Dwayne into the residential tent. "The layout's pretty simple. Available, deflated air mattresses are over there in the corner. Clean blankets, pillows, and pillow cases are sitting next to them. Open spots are obvious. Five people sleep perpendicular to the left, right, and far wall. Pick an empty spot and organize however you want. If you have any questions, just ask someone. Nobody's going to bite your head off, and everyone here can relate to what you're going through with it being your first day 'n all—everybody's had one. Some just survived it a little better than others, didn't they Jake?"

Jake's head popped up from behind the book he was reading. "And just what do you mean by that?"

"Oh, I see! So now you're just going to pretend it never happened, huh?"

"I have no idea what you're talking about, sergeant."

"Pffft! Okay, if you say so, buddy-boy! Anyways, going around counter-clockwise, there's Jake, Brad, Cleadus, Zachre,

Wolfe, Wille, Dee, Lewis, Morris, and Doug. Guys, this is James and Dwayne. You all have about fifteen minutes of personal time left, and then we'll meet in the main tent for class. You boys get settled in, and I'll see you in a little while," Sergeant Courtney said, walking out of the tent.

"Do you really go by James?" the individual who had been reading asked. "Or do you prefer 'Jim,' or 'Jimmy'?"

"'James' is fine. And who are you again?"

"Jake."

"I thought so, but I wasn't sure. The sergeant went through the introductions pretty fast."

"Don't worry, you'll catch on to everyone's name sooner or later."

"Hey, what did the sergeant mean when he said, 'some just survive their first day a little better than others'? What happened on your first day here?"

"Nothing!" Jake buried his head back in his book. "Nothing happened."

"Aw, bullshit!" Brad hollered. "C'mon Jake, tell the story! It gets funnier every time I hear it!"

"Yo, Jake!" Morris laughed. "Tell it just one more time! Then we won't ask you no more!"

"That's what you said the last *three* times we had new people show up."

"Yo! Seriously! This'll really be the final time, for real!"

"But I don't even remember doing it. One of you tell it, if you want to hear it so bad!"

"Okay!" Willie thrust his hand in the air. "I'll tell it!"

"You?"! Dee cut him off. "You weren't here to see it! You just heard about it. I saw it live! I'll tell it!"

"Oh, brother." Jake sunk deeper behind his reading material.

"Alright, get this!" Dee said. "We was all in here just chillin' after our second shift of field work, right, and Jake was laying there reading like he was when you came in. Then, for no reason at all, he put his book down and started looking all around the room, way up in the air. I thought he was watching a fly or something. But none of us saw no flies, so Doug crept over to him and asked what he was watching. Jake leaned in real close to him and whispered, 'baby gophers.'

"Dude! Doug looked shocked as shit! He said, 'what?'! And Jake said real quiet, 'Yeah. Evil little fury bastards.' Then, like a shot, Jake leaped off his bed and ran out of the tent, screaming bloody murder!"

"No way!" James exclaimed.

"Oh, yeah! But hold on! It gets better! With him yelling like that, Sgt. Courtney came out of his tent to see what was going on. And just as we was telling him what happened, here come Jake tippy-toeing out of the supply tent, butt-ass naked, wearing his underwear on his head like a helmet!

"The sarge screamed, 'Boy, what in the hell are you doing? And why are you naked?'! Jake ran up to him—and with his underwear now covering one of his eyes—he saluted him and hollered, 'Sir, the tiny flying gophers! They shot me with their little flamethrowers and caught my clothes on fire, so I had to undress!' And then he ran back in our tent and hid under his air mattress!"

"Oh my God, that's the funniest story I ever heard!" James howled.

"Not to me!" Jake said.

"Oh, I'm sorry, Jake. Do you know what made you flip out like that?"

"Yeah. I have what's called 'amphetamine psychosis.' It comes from doing too much crystal meth over the years. Cleadus and Zachre have it too. It causes us to hear voices and hallucinate sometimes. Cleadus played a game of checkers the other day with a leprechaun, and Zachre recently put a counselor in a headlock, thinking he was a creature from outer space.

"Sgt. Courtney said that our episodes will end after a few months, but until the shit gets out of our systems, pretty much anything can happen."

"Ding-ding-ding-ding-ding!"

"What was that?" Dwayne asked.

"That was good ol' Sergeant Courtney. His wife bought him an antique bell from some auction last week, and he brought it out here to use, to call us to class and field work."

"Oh, like schoolhouses used to ring back in the old days."

"Yup. The sarge has to be one of the most unique men I ever met. I saw him help a kid put a Band-Aid on once. And I also saw him body slam someone once. All in all though, he's a good dude. It's cool that he actually cares. None of my other counselors ever gave a shit about me. He does though. Come on, we better get going. You don't want to be late for your first session of field work. He doesn't tolerate tardiness. He'll send your ass home in a heartbeat."

"Shit! Come on then, let's go!"

24

"**B**rad, number four. Willie, you get number eight.
Dee, number five." Sgt. Courtney issued
uniquely numbered pickaxes to the men the
following morning. "Alright, listen up! This is the only shift of
field work we're going to have today, so make it a good one.
Hopefully, we'll get lucky and find some coal. But either way,
we're packing up this afternoon and moving to a new location.

"You men have put forth a diligent effort over the past
month, but I feel this site's become stale, so we're going to try
someplace different. Make sure you have your antivenin kit and at
least one bottle of water to take down into the pit with you, and
have a safe dig."

James and Dwayne thought there would be additional
instructions, but Sgt. Courtney simply turned around and headed
back to his tent.

Dwayne gawked at the pit and scratched his head.

Then, very cautiously, he began to descend its steep slope.

Tiny pebbles rolled out from under his lug sole and
tumbled down incline as if they were miniature boulders.

Sometimes his foot would ride on top of them, forcing him to freeze in place until he regained his balance.

"Your name's Dwayne, right?" He heard someone call out.

"Yea-yea-yeah," he replied, flailing his arms, trying not to fall.

"Hold still a minute. Just stay put till I get there."

He had no idea who was coming down to meet him, but the advice of 'not moving' sounded like a good idea at the time.

A few seconds later, Doug strolled by, puttering along the precarious hillside like he was part mountain goat. "First time in the pit can be a bit dicey." He smirked. "Give me your pickax. I'll hold it for you so you don't sock yourself in the face with it when you fall."

"*When* I fall? Don't you mean, '*if*'?"

"Well, being that this is your first run, I'd say that 'when' is more accurate, but we'll see. Here, watch me. I'll show you a trick. Look at my feet. See? Don't take normal steps; walk more on your heels when you're not on flat ground. And put a little extra oomph into each step, to make the back corner of your sole sink into the sand when you walk."

Dwayne put extra pressure on his heels each time he took a step, and he cruised on down to the bottom of the pit with ease. "Hey, cool! That worked. Thanks."

"No problem. Here's your pickax back. You can work wherever you like, but if you dig next to someone, it makes the time go by faster."

"Can I dig next to you?"

"Sure. Follow me." He led Dwayne over to where he'd been working, and they began to dig. "So, how'd you sleep last night?"

"Not too bad."

"That's good. A lot of guys have a rough first night. They told you about shaking out your sheets, right?"

"Shaking out my sheets? No. What do you mean?"

"Whenever you take a break or go to bed, always shake your sheets out before you lie down, to make sure there's no desert spiders, snakes, or scorpions hiding in your bedding."

"Scorpions! No, no one told me anything about shaking squat!"

"Yeah, this is one place that you want to make sure you're sleeping alone, or you could end up having a really bad night."

"Yeah, I'd say!" Dwayne suddenly felt like there were thousands of venomous bugs crawling all over his body.

Resting his pickax on the ground, he briskly rubbed himself all over.

Given how he was swatting himself and jiggling around, he didn't hear Zachre walk up behind him.

The wild-eyed individual observed Dwayne's erratic behavior from merely a foot away. Then he leaned in even closer to him. "You can feel it too, can't ya?" he whispered in Dwayne's ear.

"AHHHH-SHIT!!" Dwayne screamed, involuntarily thrusting his pelvis forward, rising up on the balls of his feet. "What in the hell is your problem?"!

Zachre didn't back away. He didn't even flinch. All he did was raise his eyebrows and repeat himself. "You can feel it seeping in through your skin like me, can't ya?" He wore a wicked grin. "Looks like it's making you itchy. Sometimes it makes me itchy, too."

"What?"! Dwayne shrieked. "Making me itchy? What are you talking about?"!

"The radiation." He gestured toward Dwayne's torso. "That's what's making you claw at yourself like you're doing."

"Radiation? There's no radiation out here... Is there?"

"Sure!" Zachre replied. "It's all over the place. There's over a thousand mines nearby, and they're all oozing with radiation. Sometimes it's so thick, I can see it hanging in the air like fog does."

"You can't *see* radiation!" Dwayne said.

"I can too."

"Okay, first off, that's impossible. And secondly, there's no way that ARCS would make us dig for coal in a dangerous environment."

"Pffft! Coal! We ain't digging for coal. That's just what they tell us. Think about it!"

"Think about what?"

"Alien ships, man! They put us expendable criminals out here, smack-dab in the middle of Uraniumville, to scour this radioactive wasteland for wrecked spaceships and the remains of creatures, because no one else will! Why do you think they got us working so close to Area 51 and Roswell, New Mexico?"

"Because we— It's so that—" Dwayne scratched his head as he looked around. "Hey, we *are* close to both of them, aren't we?"

"Yup. And if the radiation makes us so sick that we croak, they pay off the doctors to falsify our autopsy reports."

"They what?"!

"That's right. Your autopsy report will say that you were a drug addict who relapsed and died from an overdose. It won't mention the word, 'radiation,' at all. That way, no one will ever catch on to their diabolical plan."

"Whose diabolical plan? Who are 'they'?"!

Zachre rolled his eyes. "The government, man! You know, secret sects of the FBI, NSA, CIA—"

"Yeah," Doug said. "And the LOL, the OMG, and the IDC. We know, Zachre, we know. And do you know *how* we know?"

"No, how?"

Doug looked around, pretending to ensure no one else was within listening distance. "Because Dwayne and I are *spies* for them!" he whispered.

"Spies?"! Zachre clambered up the side of the pit on all fours like a rabid animal frothing at the mouth.

"Well, that was one way to get rid of his stupid ass!" Doug laughed.

"Not exactly the nicest way." Dwayne chuckled. "But it worked."

By the time Sgt. Courtney blew his whistle, signaling the end of the shift, Dwayne felt like he was going to keel over. Despite being in the midst of executing a powerful downswing when it sounded, the virgin miner's muscles turned to mush before the tiny wooden ball inside the sergeant's antique little noisemaker made its third reverberation.

"Whew!" Dwayne stumbled to his left.

"Are you tired?" Doug chortled.

"I— I'm pooped!"

"Eh, you'll get used to it. Grab your empty water bottle, and let's get out of here. Did you get assigned your relocation tasks yet?"

"Yeah. I'm in charge of deflating and bundling the air mattresses, and packing up all the linen."

"That's cool. You'll be fine. All the plastic storage bins are labeled, so it's pretty self-explanatory. It'll be nice to move to a new spot. I'm ready for a change of scenery."

"Change of scenery? Isn't it all the same, no matter where we go?"

"No. There are differences. This location is bleak and boring."

"Oh, I don't know... Some of the rock formations around here are big enough to hide behind; that's a nice amenity."

Doug looked at him. "How's a boulder an amenity?"

"Because both latrines were occupied this morning, and I really had to pee, so I went behind one of them."

"Well, even with your makeshift urinal, this location sucks compared to some of the other places we've been to."

"What was so special about them?"

"Dude, it was awesome! As soon as we walked out of our tent in the morning, the first thing we saw was two big buttes. And there were cacti everywhere, with delicious tuna hanging off them! I'm telling you, that was—" Doug noticed that Dwayne had stopped walking some time ago. He was about twenty feet back, standing still. "Dwayne? What's wrong?"

"Oh, I'm fine," he replied. "The question is, 'how are *you*?'"

"I'm hot and thirsty, but other than that, I'm fine. Why?"

"Because you just said that you saw two butts, and fish hanging from cacti. Being honest, you sound a lot like Zachre. I tell you what, why don't you go on ahead of me, and I'll catch up with you in a little bit."

"Get up here, you dumbbell!" Doug laughed. "I guess that did sound a little weird, didn't it? No, I saw two 'buttes,' not 'butts.' Buttes are humongous rock formations; they look like 300-foot-tall skyscrapers sticking up out of the ground."

"And what about the fish?"

"Not fish. 'Tuna.' Tuna is another name for a cactus pear. It's a prickly red fruit that grows on certain cacti. You can eat them. They're good."

"Oh. I was beginning to think that you suffered from amphetamine psychosis too, and just didn't tell anyone."

"No. I have my fair share of issues, but none of them entail pummeling monsters from Mars or fleeing from fire-breathing gophers."

"Well, that's a plus."

Over the next ninety minutes, the crew operated like a well-oiled machine, boxing up everything in sight.

"Is it empty yet?"! Sgt. Courtney yelled, referring to the main residential tent.

"Yes, sir," Brad replied.

"Are both front flaps tied open, to let the air escape?"

"One is. Hold on. I'm getting the other side now."

"Okay. Good. Now I need three guys at each corner; one at the base of the poles, and one at each of the guide rope anchors. Veterans, brief the new guys on what to do. We go on 'three.' Ready? One... two..."

"No, wait!" Morris yelled. "Yo, Sarge! We only got two people on this corner!"

"That doesn't make sense," Sgt. Courtney replied. "Three guys at four corners equals twelve people, and I got twelve of you guys out here with me."

"Someone might be in the bathroom or something."

"Alright. Hold on Morris, I'm coming."

Sgt. Courtney hustled over to the unmanned peg and prepared to pull it from the ground. "Okay, on three! One... two... three! Weigh the anchors and batten down the hatches!"

The men extracted the tent stakes and pushed the tops of the corner supports toward the center of the tent, to ensure they fell inward.

In no time at all, the unit's living quarters imploded, until it had become flat enough to fold into a compact bundle.

As they waited on all the air to escape, Brad noticed Dwayne chuckling. "What's so funny?" he asked.

"I didn't expect the sarge to have such a slick sense of humor, that's all."

"Why? What did he say?"

"Didn't you hear him? He used a clever nautical idiom, and we're in the middle of the *desert*!"

"He what?"

"He ordered us to 'weigh the anchor and batten down the hatches.' Get it? Captains at sea give that order when they want the boat anchor raised, whereas the sarge gave it to us in the desert, alluding to the tent stakes. See the irony?"

"Yeah, I see it."

"Don't you find it funny?"

"Yeah, it's funny. But whenever a joke has to be explained, it sort of ruins the chances of it being 'laugh-out-loud' funny."

"Good point. You know, I remember once when I—"

"Do you know what I find funny?"! A hostile voice growled, storming into their conversation. "I find it funny that everyone else is busting their ass in the blazing heat, packing up all our equipment and supplies, while you two cutie-pies take time to chat and get to know each other! I mean, shit! Why don't you just hold hands, whack each other off, and get it over with all ready? Or maybe you'd like me to bring you a bottle of wine first... with your Dishonorable Discharge Papers!"

Brad and Dwayne launched into apologies.

"Shut up!" The sergeant yelled. "Now go find someone who looks like they know what they're doing, and ask them how you can help! Now! Go! Get out of my sight!"

25

"Alright guys," Sgt. Courtney said. "Good job getting everything packed up and loaded. Now gather round so I can get a quick head count, and then we'll get going." The sergeant stood up on the truck bumper to gain an advantageous view. "... nine... ten... eleven... Stand still guys. I know it's hot, but stop fidgeting and moving around. I must have missed someone."

Sgt. Courtney counted a second time. And once again, he came up short. "Dammit! Who's missing?"!

Everyone looked around.

"Zachre," James replied. "Where's Zachre?"

From his elevated position, the sergeant scanned the group. "You're right. He's not here. Okay, listen up! Did Zachre talk to any of you about fleeing or hurting himself?"

No one said anything.

"Well, we'll give him ten minutes to show up, and if he doesn't join us by then, I'll report him missing. Either way, we're moving on. In the meantime, y'all can hang out here, or you can jump in the back of one of the canopied trucks, where it should be a little cooler."

Dwayne walked to the closest truck and climbed into the back of it with a bottle of water. Brad was already inside. "Do you mind if I ride along with you?" Dwayne asked.

"No, be my guest. So, who did you end up helping, after we got yelled at?"

"Morris. How about you?"

"Willie."

"How'd everything go?" Dwayne asked, examining the skin between his thumb and first finger.

"Fine. What's wrong with your hand?"

"The handle of the pickax gave me a blister."

"Yeah, you'll get those the first week or two. They'll burn like hell for a while, and then they'll turn into calluses. After that, you'll be fine."

"You're definitely right about it hurting." He pressed on it. "It's tight."

"So drain it."

"How?"

"Bite it."

"Ewww, yuck! No!"

"Oh, don't be a wuss. Use your front teeth, and bite through the dead skin so the fluid can drain out."

"The skin that's raised up is dead?"

"Yup."

"So it won't hurt if I bite it?"

"Nope."

Dwayne studied his hand for a few more seconds. With a high degree of skepticism, he raised it to his mouth.

But as soon as he felt the miniature epidermal mound touch the tip of his tongue, he jerked his hand away from his face. "Are you sure it's not going to hurt?"!

Brad laughed at him. "I'm sure."

Dwayne returned his hand to his lips, situated the fleshy bulge between his incisors and bit through what felt like the edge of a watermelon seed, allowing the fluid to escape. "Hey, that *does* feel better."

"See, I told you."

"Hey, guys." Dee poked his head in the back of the truck.

"What's up, man?" Brad said. "You want to ride with us?"

"No. I was actually wondering if you two wanted to ride with me and James. I'm going to go over some of the ins and outs of how we operate; you know, teach him some of the shit I had to learn the hard way. How about it? You guys want to join us?"

"I don't know... maybe." Dwayne looked at Brad. "Are you?"

"I appreciate the invitation, but I'm good," he replied. "You can go if you want to, though."

Dwayne scratched the side of his face, looked at Dee, and then turned his attention back to Brad. Then he set his water down, bumping his blister. "Owww!" He clutched his hand.

"Look, I'm gonna head back! If you want to ride with us, come join us before we leave," Dee said, walking away. "If not, that's cool too."

Sitting across from Dwayne, Brad took advantage of having the bench seat to himself by lying down on it. He was in the shade, and to his surprise, quite comfortable. There was even a gentle breeze swirling around under the canopy of the truck.

Taking immense appreciation in the rare moment of sereneness, he put a towel over his face, took a deep breath, and closed his eyes.

Just then, Dwayne knocked over his water. "Dammit!"

"Ahh!" Brad sat straight up. "What the hell's wrong with you?"!

"Nothing. I just spilt my water. Sorry about making you jump. Hey, listen. I'm going to go grab another one, and then I'm going to hitch a ride with Dee and James. You go ahead and catch some Z's, and I'll see you when we get to the next site, okay?"

"Uh-huh." Brad closed his eyes and lay back down.

Dwayne jumped out of the truck and headed toward the vehicle that had the bottled water on board. But no sooner had he started walking than a big boulder caught his eye. "Hmmm." He stared at it. "Maybe I should take one final leak before we leave."

Running over to it, Dwayne darted around back to conceal himself from everyone, unzipped his fly, and began urinating.

But before he finished, he noticed a gathering of white material next to him.

Unable to wait until he was done peeing, he sidestepped a few feet to get a better look. Something was underneath it.

"Za—" Dwayne began to say Zachre's name, but then whirled around when he realized he was still holding his penis.

After making himself presentable, he turned back around. Zachre?" he whispered, trepidation clear in his voice.

"Yeah?" Zachre replied from under the sheet as if nothing was out of the ordinary.

Dwayne breathed a sigh of relief. "What are you doing, bud?"

"I'm hiding from Uranium Agents."

"Zachre, listen. There's nobody around here except you and me, and everyone else is packed up and ready to leave. Come on. I'll take you to Sgt. Courtney. We have to go."

"Sergeant Courtney?" Zachre said, sticking his head out from under the sheet. Squinting and blinking, he waited on his eyes to adjust to the brightness. Then he got a good look at Dwayne. "Oh, no! You're that spy!" he shouted, grasping a baseball-size rock off the ground.

"No, Doug was just kidding." Dwayne chortled. "I'm not a—"

Suddenly, Zachre slugged him in the side of the head with the rock, knocking him unconscious.

Dwayne collapsed behind the boulder, and Zachre took off. "Wait!" he screamed, falling down every few seconds as he sprinted back to the caravan. "Don't leave! I'm coming!"

"Where the hell have you been?"! Sergeant Courtney scorned him.

Despite being out of breath, Zachre did his best to reply. "I— I fighting spies!"

"Oh, brother! I sure will be glad when you're done having your episodes, Zachre."

"Huh?" He continued panting.

"Nothing! Just get in the damn truck!"

Once he was inside, Sgt. Courtney whistled up to the driver, who leaned out of the cab and looked back. "You ready, Sarge?"

"Yeah, we got everybody now. Let's go! We're burning daylight!"

"Ah'ight!" He fired up the engine and pulled away, the rest of the fleet following suit.

26

"Uuuh," Dwayne moaned as he regained consciousness.

He attempted to stand; sharp pains shot through the base of his skull. Clenching his teeth, he struggled to his feet.

He looked down at his shirtsleeve. It was encrusted with blood. And his head was throbbing. But what troubled him most was that he had no idea where he was, or how he got there.

Alternating feet, he dragged them through the scorching sand in a westerly direction, gaping at the distant horizon as if it were an attainable destination.

Then reality set in. Sheer panic flooded every cell in his body. "Calm down, Dwayne. Get ahold of yourself. Now *think*."

Although he couldn't help but to ponder how he ended up covered in blood, in the middle of the desert, he knew he must focus. Assuming he couldn't be too far from civilization, Dwayne ventured into the unforgiving wilderness just as the topmost point of the sun sank below the skyline.

27

Several hours into his journey, Dwayne was faring rather well. His headache had subsided, the temperature hadn't dropped all that low, and he was hustling along at a pretty good clip.

The problem was that he had no idea whether he was heading in the direction of a populous community, or trekking deeper into the desert.

As time passed, his uneventful walk lent him a false sense of security. He even began taking in the scenery, which was being illuminated by a full moon.

Just then, he noticed a pair of voles hopping around up ahead, playing among clusters of sandstone.

"Hey guys," he whispered, making his way over to them. "Come on, don't be afraid."

The two little furballs scampered over to the opposite side of a hoodoo, where they rekindled their roughhousing.

Dwayne crept up to the rock, stooped down, and peeped around the corner to spy on them.

In order to draw their attention without frightening them, he mimicked the sounds they were making by repetitively sucking the tip of his tongue off the roof of his mouth.

Seeing that they had stopped frolicking and were looking in his direction, he outstretched his right hand to the base of the rock and flicked the sand as he continued making the noise.

To his delight, they began walking toward him—one cautious step at a time.

Dwayne smiled. The tender experience was providing just the reprieve he needed.

Placing his free hand on the rock to remain balanced on the balls of his feet, he continued wriggling his fingers around in the sand.

Soon, they were so close, he could see their whiskers.

He watched them sniff the crisp night air.

Then they froze.

"No, don't stop," Dwayne whispered, wanting to touch their fur, or better yet, maybe even pet them. "Just two more inches, guys. Come on, you can— SHIT!" A deadly snake sprung out of the rocks, and thrust its venomous fangs into one of the voles.

Dwayne scrambled backwards, dragging his buttocks on the ground along the way. Gasping for air and trembling with fear, he watched in horror as the predator writhed around its kill.

28

5:47 am

Twilight would be giving birth to the new day's dawn at any moment.

Dwayne had been walking all night. He was tired, thirsty, and dreading the inevitable increase in temperature.

But he had no choice but to keep going.

He thought he would have come across a small town or a service station by daybreak. But he was wrong.

And then it happened: that God-awful ball of infernal heat crested the horizon. "No!" he cried out.

Although his body was capable of tolerating the sun, his mind was not. "Just fucking rise, already! Go ahead! You know you're going to!" he screamed, knowing he would be tortured by its blistering rays for the remainder of the day, until it ultimately killed him.

But then he had a thought—a thought so profound that it caused him to stop and gaze upon the sun in *awe*: this may be the *last* sunrise he'll ever see.

After all, he had no food, no water, and there was no shade in sight.

That being realized, Dwayne stood still and drank in the glorious spectacle for a few minutes, before pressing on.

29

4:23 pm

Over and over again, Dwayne summoned up what he believed was his last ounce of strength, dragging his leaden feet through the searing sand, merely four inches at a time.

It hurt to breathe, his muscles ached, and grotesque blisters covered his skin.

He fell to his knees and remained erect for a moment, wavering on his shins. But then he collapsed even further so that his buttocks rested on his heels.

His head wobbled atop his torso as if it were held in place by a rubber band.

He surveyed the vast wasteland. "How?" he wondered. "How is this possible? Nothing but sand as far as the eye can see. So— so hot. Hurt— so bad."

He tried to swallow, but he couldn't. There was no moisture in his mouth. The sweltering heat and dry desert air had ravaged his trachea, leaving his entire respiratory system in critical condition.

Suddenly, his left hamstring drew into a horrendous cramp, toppling him into the jagged grains of sand face-first.

Using his last bit of energy, he pulled his hand up from where it lay by his thigh to shade his eyes.

Exhaling what he hoped would be his final breath, he begged for mercy. "God, please forgive me for all my sins and bring me home. Please. Just let me die."

Still in agony, Dwayne opened his eyes only to see that nothing had happened. He was still alive.

Once again, he pleaded for relief in the form of a swift death. "Lord God, please hear my calling and come to my rescue. What have I done to deserve this? I beg of you, please let me die."

But once again, nothing happened.

Incapable of moving, he shut his eyes and waited on the inevitable.

30

9:33 pm

The sun descended behind the horizon, giving way to a clear, starlit evening. Dwayne was neither in pain nor dead. He was unconscious.

Off in the distance, the cry of a lone coyote broke the silence of the night.

A scorpion picked up on Dwayne's presence. It approached his kneecap.

Unimpressed with its findings, it meandered toward his face.

But the scorpion was not the only creature honing in on Dwayne's body. For another entity was making its way to him: a man on horseback.

The scorpion stopped beside Dwayne's throat. It reared its venom-tipped tail and prepared to strike, but the stranger's thunderous arrival broke its concentration.

The man approached. The arachnid whirled around and thrust its poisonous stinger into his ankle.

Although the attack was executed with tremendous force and precision, it had no chance of piercing the individual's thick leather boot.

The man's counterattack consisted of nothing more than a sweeping motion of his foot, propelling the little critter several yards leftward, where it landed unhurt and out of the way.

In no time, the agile stranger had lifted Dwayne's body off the sand, draped him over his horse, and rode off into the night.

31

Opening his eyes, Dwayne found himself lying on his back, looking up at logs and dried mud. Surrounded by soil and timber, he appeared to be in some kind of hut with a doorway built into the wall.

Then, in his peripheral vision, he saw something move: a man was crouched down just a few feet away, facing the opposite direction.

Hearing Dwayne stir precipitated him to stand up and turn around. It was a Native American Indian. His hands and feet were painted snow-white, and atop his head, there sat an animal skull.

Dwayne's eyes locked onto his, his heart racing.

The Navajo approached. "Be still," he said in a deep voice, dabbing Dwayne's face with a cool wet cloth.

Then he poured some water into a glass, inserted a straw, and placed the end of it between Dwayne's cracked, blood-caked lips. "Try to drink. Not too much. Only little."

Dwayne drew the water up the straw and into his mouth, grimacing each time he swallowed.

"That enough." The Indian extracted it from his mouth. "Too much make you sick. You rest now."

Walking back over to his sandpainting, he knelt down and continued working on it as he chanted. The Navajo shaman was in the midst of conducting an ancient healing ritual, in an effort to save Dwayne's life.

32

Roused from a deep sleep by the sound of crooning and scraping, Dwayne awoke to the shaman mixing something inside a small clay bowl.

Sensing Dwayne's heightened state of awareness, the old man looked up at him and nodded.

After a little more stirring and grinding, the Indian ambled over to him, took a seat, and leaned in close to examine his wretched complexion. Raising his eyebrows, he tilted his head to the right, to the left, and then back to the right again.

Finally—without looking away from Dwayne's face—the shaman pressed two of his fingers into the bowl, swirled them around until they were covered in slime, and then reached out.

Up to that point, Dwayne was merely curious as to what he was doing. But seeing two fingers full of green goo coming at him was more than he could handle. "Huh-uh!" He smashed his head deeper into his pillow, in a futile attempt to evade the greasy-looking glob.

The shaman, who was now dressed in traditional Navajo Indian garb, alleviated his worries. "Shhh, Running Bird," he said in a soft voice. "You be still now. This just medicine."

"Running Bird? Who's Running Bird?" Dwayne furrowed his brow, so distracted by the comment that he didn't feel the gel being slathered onto his forehead and cheeks.

Then the Indian handed him a plate of porridge and boiled squash. "Here, eat," he said.

Dwayne looked at the soft food that had been prepared for him, but that's all he did—was just *look* at it.

"What wrong?" the shaman asked. "You no hungry?"

With a pitiful expression, Dwayne pointed to his throat. He moved his mouth, but no words came out.

"What you say? I can't hear you."

Sighing in disgust, Dwayne grasped the man's collar and pulled downward.

The Indian bent over.

"Can't eat," Dwayne whispered, grimacing terribly. "Hurts just to talk."

Without saying a word, the shaman took the bowl out of his hands, placed it on the shelf, and inhaled a deep, cleansing breath.

Then he stood up, closed his eyes, and raised his arms out from his sides.

"What in the world is he doing now?" Dwayne wondered.

But he didn't have to wonder for long. For the shaman thrust his hands forward and slammed his palms together. Soon, they began vibrating. Then a faint glow appeared between them as if he'd wrapped his fingers around a light bulb.

Suddenly, his eyes popped wide open, and his left hand shot out and wrapped itself around Dwayne's throat.

Panic-stricken and paralyzed, the injured young man was forced to tolerate what felt like surges of electricity being pushed into his body. Finally, the shaman let go.

"What in the hell is your problem?"! Dwayne yelled. "I got no beef with you! Why are you trying to choke me? You're gonna—" His eyes widened with amazement. "Hey! I can talk. And my throat doesn't hurt anymore. What— what did you do to me?"

The elderly Indian gawked at him. "What about a beef?" he muttered, scrunching his eyebrows together. "Snakes out here in desert. Lots of snakes and lizards. No beef."

"Huh? No. It's just an expression. 'I got no beef with you.' It means, like, 'we don't have any problems between us.' You know, 'I like you.'"

The shaman smiled. "Ah, that good!" He handed Dwayne his plate again. "I like you too, Running Bird. Here, eat. Help you get strength back."

"Thanks. Hey, wait. You never said how you fixed my voice. Where am I, anyways? And who are you? What's your name?"

"You in my hogan. I live here. My name, Rising Water." He topped off Dwayne's glass. "*Chief* Rising Water. You want straw in drink?"

"No, fank 'ou." Dwayne replied, shoveling food in his mouth after not having eaten for days. "Why are you calling me Running Bird? And how did you—"

"Shhh. We talk later. You be still now. And slow up eating. You get sick if you eat too fast." The chief made his way to the door. "And don't try to stand up. You just rest now. Maybe try stand up tomorrow. I be back in little bit." He said, walking outside, leaving Dwayne alone to enjoy his meal.

33

"Ah, good morning, Running Bird," Chief Rising Water said, taking down the blanket that was hanging the doorway. "How'd you sleep?"

"Ehh!" Dwayne shaded his eyes. "Good, until you let the sun into your little mud-hut just now."

"This not a mud-hut. It called a 'hogan.'"

"A hogan? I thought all Indians lived in teepees."

"Eh, you watch too much TV." The old man huffed. "Only tribes ever lived in teepees were Great Plains tribes, where there used to be many buffalo. Need a buffalo hide to make a teepee. Tribes in southwest live in hogans and wickiups. Nowadays though, most Indians choose to live in modern home and have fancy lifestyle. But not me."

"So, is that where I am?" Dwayne sat up in bed. "The southwest?"

"Yes. Arizona."

"How did I get here?"

Rising Water sat down beside him. "I get you from desert. Then I bring you back here."

"So how do I get home?"

"I don't know. Where you from?"

"I'm from— I'm from... um..." Dwayne's eyes became huge, his heart pounding in his chest. "I don't know! What do I do now? I can't remember! How am I—"

"Shhh, Running Bird. You be still. Your memory will come back when it's ready. You just—"

"But Mr. Rushing River! I can't even remember my name!"

"First of all, my name 'Rising Water,' not 'Rushing River.'"

"Oh, sorry."

"That okay. Now listen. When time is right, you will remember everything." He placed his hand on Dwayne's shoulder. "Don't worry. Worrying not going to do any good, anyhow. So why do it? Okay?"

"Okay."

"Until then, you have honorary Navajo Indian name of 'Running Bird.' For now, just be thankful you not all sprawled out dead in desert; you *alive*. *And* you have place to live. Here. With me. Must appreciate what you *do* have in life. Then you be happy. See? Could be lots worse, right?"

Dwayne thought for a moment. "Yeah. You're right."

"Ah, very good!" The chief hopped up from his seated position like a man half his age. "You stay put. Drink some more water. I fix us breakfast. Then we stand you up, and see how you do walking around. I be back in little bit," he said, heading toward the doorway.

"Excuse me, Chief?" Running Bird called to him.

Rising Water stopped and turned around. "Yes? Something wrong?"

"No, sir. I just wanted to thank you for taking care of me. You— you saved my life."

"Ah, my pleasure, Running Bird." He smiled. "My pleasure indeed."

34

"Okay, let's see if you can stand," Rising Water said. "Try moving feet off cot, and onto floor."

Running Bird sat up, turned sideways, and eased his legs off the bed. Then he drew in a short breath, held it, and stood up.

"There you go! How's that feel?"

"Fine." He smiled, flexing his knees.

"Good. Now, very gently, squat whole way down. Then stand up again."

Running Bird crouched down and stood back up. "Hey, that was easy!" he said, taking a few steps to boot. "While I'm up, I'm going to go outside and take a leak. What do you do around here, just go behind a rock?"

"No. Stand out in open."

"Out in the open? That'll feel kind of weird. Why can't I go behind a rock?"

"General rule is, 'don't stick anything behind rock that you'd miss, if something jumps out and bites it off.'"

Running Bird's face lost all expression. "Well, out it in the open, it is!"

When he returned from urinating, Rising Water was nowhere to be found. "Hey, Chief!" Running Bird hollered. "Where'd you go?"

"Back here. I behind hogan, in wickiup."

Running Bird walked around back. "Whoa! They're beautiful!"

"What beautiful?" the chief asked, emerging from the wickiup with a saddle. "Oh, you see horses. Yes, they very nice. Very gentle."

"What are their names?"

"'Thunder' and 'Lightning.'"

"Aw, cool names! Which one's which?"

"Thunder is the darker one. She's the one you'll be riding."

"Who, me? I don't know how to ride horses!"

"You worry too much. Go in wickiup and bring out other saddle. I show you what to do."

"Me? Are you sure?"

"Yes. You go now. Get saddle."

Running Bird lumbered into the wickiup and retrieved the other saddle.

"Good. Now take these." Rising Water handed him a bag of baby carrots. "Go feed Thunder. Give her one or two at a time."

"Feed her? How?"

"Hold hand out, and keep it flat, like this." He showed him. "See? Nothing to it. She's just like people but with four legs."

"She's a lot bigger than people!"

The chief chuckled. "You go feed her now. I get more supplies, and be back in a minute."

"Uh, okay. If you say so." Running Bird made his way over to the giant creature, his walk slowing as he neared her.

He stood by Thunder's front leg and peered up at her face.

The horse blinked and swished her tail.

Swallowing the lump in his throat, Running Bird reached into his bag. "Would you like some carrots?" he asked softly, pulling out two. "Here you go." He placed them under her nose.

Thunder picked them up with her lips and pulled them into her mouth. "Crunch, crunch, crunch." She enjoyed her treat.

Running Bird gazed at the massive mammal in awe. "You're incredible," he whispered as he pet her. "Do you want some more? Okay, hold on. They're sorta small, aren't they? Here ya go."

Once again, she removed them from his palm and chewed them with delight.

Then she lowered her head farther to see who was feeding her. With the two of their faces now merely inches apart, and the sun perched at just the right point in the heavens, Running Bird froze in place. For in the center of Thunder's humongous, jet-black pupil existed his *own* reflection. How, he had no idea. But there he was—in brilliant color—peering back out at himself, from inside the eye of the magnificent animal.

And standing inside the wickiup, keeping quiet and out of sight, Chief Rising Water watched from afar, basking in the moment just as much as Running Bird was.

35

"You ride real good, Running Bird. You a quick learner." The chief complimented him as they rode alongside each other, admiring the breathtaking sunrise.

"Thank you."

"You been pretty quiet since we left hogan. You okay?"

"Yeah, I'm just a little overwhelmed by everything right now. I mean, here I am riding across the desert on a horse with an Indian, wearing a goofy black-and-white striped outfit; and to top it all off, I don't even know who I am."

"I understand."

Running Bird watched the sand kick up from Lightning's hooves as they moseyed along. "But do you know what the weirdest part is?"

"No. What?"

"I'm okay with it. Well, maybe not 'okay,' but I'm not freaking out or going nuts, inside. I don't understand why I'm not more anxious than what I am. Do you know what I mean?"

"Yes. I do. Navajo tribe call it 'harmony.' Harmony very important. For many centuries, we strive to achieve balance by living what we call, 'the good way.' You a very lucky man to have such harmony. Inner peace is very good, Running Bird. Yes, you very lucky."

"I guess." He looked off into the distance. "So, where are we headed, anyways?"

"The river."

"The river? Do you mean to tell me there's water out here?"!

"Yes. Little Colorado River is just up ahead."

"That's awesome!"

"Yes, river is very close to hogan. I like to visit this time of day. Not too cold. And not too hot. Temperature may rise eighty degrees in just eight hours here later. Must be careful not to—"

"Eighty degrees in eight hours! That sucks!"

The chief furrowed his brow. "Sucks? What you mean, 'sucks'?"

"'That sucks.' It's an expression that people use when something bad happens."

Rising Water glared at him.

"What's wrong?" Running Bird asked.

"You sure talk funny," the chief replied. "Got no cows with me. Stuff sucking. I wish you just talk normal, so I understand you."

"Got no cows with me?" Running Bird murmured, blinking a couple times. Then his eyes lit up. "Oh! 'I got no *beef* with you!'"

"Yeah, that's right."

"Okay." Running Bird laughed. "I'll try to watch how I phrase things. Sorry."

"That okay."

Cresting the canyon, Running Bird got his first look at the river. "Oh, wow! This is huge!"

"No. Not huge. This *Little* Colorado River. If you want huge, follow it that way forty miles." The chief pointed northwest. "That where it flows into Colorado River, closer to Grand Canyon."

"This is amazing!" Running Bird looked around from atop Thunder. "How do we get down to the water?"

"There's lots of trails. Closest one this way. Follow me." Rising Water led them to the bottom of the canyon, where the bank gradually sloped down to the river.

Right away, Thunder and Lightning began munching mounds of tall grass.

"Can we get off the horses and walk around?" Running Bird asked. "Or will they run away?"

"You can get off, but stay here a minute," Rising Water replied, dismounting Lighting. He reached into her one saddle bag and pulled out a towel and a bar of soap. "Here! You go take bath now. You stink."

"Take a *bath*? Where? Out there in the river?"!

The chief peered over the top of Running Bird's shoulder, looked out at the river for a second, and then looked back at Running Bird. "Well, out there in river seems to be where all the water is, so that's where best place would be to take bath."

Running Bird snatched the soap and towel out of his hands, tromped down to the water, and began to undress. But no sooner did he take off his pants than Chief Rising Water burst out laughing harder than he'd ever laughed before. "Hey Running Bird!" he howled.

"What?"!

"Nice pair of pink underwears you have on! Real pretty!"

"Not funny, Chief! Not funny at all!" Running Bird stomped out into the river with his little bar of soap.

Then it triggered in his brain how refreshing the cool water felt against his sore body, and he forgot all about being the butt of a joke. "Aaaahhh!" He breathed out, shutting his eyes as he eased himself down into the cool water.

About a minute later, he heard the chief's voice once more. This time, however, it carried with it a soft, sincere tone. "Feels good, huh?"

Running Bird looked toward the riverbank, finding him standing at the water's edge, just a few yards away. "Oh, my!" He smiled. "You have no idea."

"Ah, very good. You take your time. Horses enjoying grass. We in no rush. It'll be a few hours yet till heat becomes unbearable. Here's new clothes for you to put on when you get out." He placed them on the ground. "I go take nap in shade now."

"Wait. New clothes? What new clothes?"

"Indian clothes. You don't want to put that striped stuff back on, do you?"

"Well, no. I just didn't expect you to have clothes for me, that's all."

"Yup. You all set. I go take nap now," he said, turning around and walking away. "Wake me when you done. Then we head back."

"Okay. Thanks, Chief."

Without turning around, Rising Water threw his hand in the air as an acknowledgement of Running Bird's "thank you" as he continued up the riverbank.

36

"Hey, Chief." Running Bird nudged his arm to awaken him. "I'm all done."

"Huh?" He sat up and rubbed his eyes. "What you say?"

"I said, 'I'm all done taking a bath.' How do I look?" Running Bird held out his arms and turned around, showing off his Indian attire.

"Hey, you look good! How everything feel? It fit okay?"

"Yeah. The shirt's really comfortable, and I love all the fringes hanging from the pants. Even the shoes are the right size."

"They not shoes. They 'teguas.'"

"Teguas? What are teguas?"

"They're what you have on your feet. Teguas are like moccasins, but taller. Teguas come up to ankles."

"Oh. Well they fit great."

"I glad you like. Looks good. Looks very good. Okay, come on. Before it gets hot out, we go upriver some and pan for a while, before we head back."

"We're going to do *what*?"

"Pan. Go get Thunder and follow me. I show you."

Riding upriver another mile or so (to where the water was shallow), the chief stopped, hopped off Lightning, and rooted around in her saddle bags. "Here." He handed Running Bird a sieve. "Take this, take off teguas, and come out in water with me."

Running Bird studied it. Then he looked out at the river. "Oh, I get it! Pan! Like, 'pan for gold.'"

"Yeah, that's right. Come on."

"Wait. Gold? You mean *real* gold? I was just using that as an example. There's no gold around here... is there? I mean, if there was gold out here, the whole country would be swarming this place, wouldn't they?"

Chief Rising Water stopped and turned around. "Think of it this way. If fisherman come across world's best place to fish but never tells anyone about it, and no one ever finds it, how many other fisherman going to be there?"

"Well, nobody because—"

"That's right, now shush! Very easy to do. You watch and learn now. Face upriver, bend down, scoop up some riverbed in pan, and shake. See?"

Putting his hand on the chief's back to steady himself, Running Bird raised his eyebrows and stretched his neck as he examined what remained in the chief's sieve. "I don't see any. Do you?"

"No, but you get the idea how to do it now, right?"

"Oh yeah, no sweat! How many times do you normally have to scoop and jiggle before you find gold?"

"It varies. Some mornings, do okay. Other times, not do so good. It just a hobby. Squatting, shaking, bending, walking against current are all very good exercise. Keep body in good shape."

"I— whoops! I— whoah!— understand." Running Bird flailed his arms as he walked through the shallows, sliding around on all the slippery rocks just below the water's surface. "Probably helps you achieve better harmony, too."

The chief rose to an erect stance, marveling at the clumsy lad's nonchalant expression of insightfulness. "Yes, Running Bird. You correct. Very well said."

"Hey, Chief! This spot looks lucky, wouldn't you say? I'm gonna try scooping— I mean, panning right here, okay?"

"Okay, but don't get discouraged if you don't find anything right away. Or even if you don't find anything at all today. It took me many, many tries before I find something. The key is to have patience. Lots and lots of patience indeed. Nobody ever finds anything on their first—"

"Holy cow! Chief, look at this!" Running Bird yelled, high stepping, hopping, and splashing his way over to his mentor. "Tah-dah!" He showed him his sieve, which contained a large gold nugget. "Ain't it great! Man, this is easy! I'm gonna go find some more!" He whirled around and stomped away, soaking Chief Rising Water in the process.

37

When they returned home, Running Bird put the saddles away, and in doing so, he noticed something he didn't see earlier in the day: vegetables were growing on the other side of the wickiup. "Hey Chief, what's that?"

"That my garden."

The young man surveyed his surroundings in every direction. Besides the garden, all that existed were a few sparse cacti. "But how do you get things to grow so nicely in that spot, when the rest of the land is barren?"

"Plants like sun, water, and good soil. Nature provides plenty of sun, and I provide water and fertilizer. Very simple."

"Oh, that makes sense. Can I go over and look at it?"

"Sure. I need to check out my weed situation, anyhow."

As they neared it, Running Bird's face squinched up. "Blachh! What's that horrible smell?"

"That's the fertilizer."

"Geesh!" He covered his mouth and nose. "What kind do you use?"!

"I use two kinds. You see all the tomato plants in the back?"

"Yeah."

"They produce lots of tomatoes. I eat what I want, and I put the rest in ground and let them rot. Rotten tomatoes make excellent fertilizer. Make soil very rich with nutrients. Grow big, juicy vegetables. The other kind is—"

"Wow, look at the size of those cucumbers over there! They're as big as my forearm! Can I pick one?"

"Sure. Just be careful where you step. Don't crush vines."

"Oh, don't worry," he replied, tiptoeing through the garden. "I'm extremely sure-footed."

"Pffft! No you not. I saw you in river. You walk around like drunken buffalo."

"Like a drunken buffalo?"! Running Bird laughed as he attempted to pick a cucumber, dragging its vine along the ground in the process.

"Be careful!" The chief scolded him.

"Well, it's not my fault! It won't let go."

"Twist it. You have to twist it to break it loose from vine, *before* you pick it up."

"Oh. Okay. {Kah-rrrunch!} Yup, that worked. I got it. Can I pick a couple more?"

"Sure. Feel free to pull up weeds while you out there, too."

"Will do. This is awesome. You should really be proud of yourself. I bet you got the best garden in all of Arizona."

The chief put his hands in his pockets and swayed to and fro, occasionally rising up on the balls of his feet as he relished in Running Bird's compliments.

"Yessiree, you sure got a green thumb!" the young man added.

All of a sudden, the chief stopped swaying. He pulled his right hand out of his pocket and examined his thumb. Seeing nothing wrong with it, he examined his other thumb. Finally, holding them side-by-side, he mumbled, "Thumbs not look green to me."

"Hey, Chief!" Running Bird shouted from his seated position in the dirt. "What's in the old tomatoes that makes the soil smell so bad?"

"Nothing," Rising Water replied, still studying his thumbs.

"What? I couldn't hear you."

"Nothing. Smell has nothing to do with tomatoes."

"Really?" Running Bird picked up a few clumps of it and squeezed, crushing them with ease. "Then what makes it stink? And why's it all lumpy?"

"Because it's dung."

"Because it's *what*?"!

"Dung. You know, from Thunder and Lightning. That's the second kind of fertilizer I use."

"Do you mean to tell me I'm sitting in horse shit?"!

"Yeah that's right. Hey, Running Bird, my thumbs don't look green to me. I don't think—"

"Oh, yuck!" Running Bird jumped up and ran out of the garden, gagging twice along the way. "Ugh! I think I'm gonna puke!" He shook, shivered, and slapped himself all over, knocking horse manure and pieces of rotten tomato in every direction. "That was—"

"SCREEEEL!!" A nearby animal belted out an ear-piercing scream, precipitating Running Bird to lunge forward and grab Rising Water around the waist. "Jeeee-sus!" He clung to the elderly Indian's waist, his wide-open eyes searching the skies. "What in the hell was that?"!

"Relax." The chief sniggered. "It just an eagle."

"An eagle?" He loosened his grip a little. "Where?"

"Up there." Rising Water pointed to the top of a nearby hoodoo. "See?"

"Aww, cool! It's huge! Are all eagles that big, or is that one special?"

The innocent inquiry induced a solemn glow of affection to radiate from the chief's face. "Oh, yes, Running Bird. Liawatha very special. Most special thing in whole world." Then he drew in a deep breath, puffed out his chest, and raised his arms until they were parallel to the ground—and amazingly, the eagle mimicked him, stretching her massive wings outward, and *holding them there*.

"But how— I mean, animals can't—" Running Bird was incapable of collecting his thoughts.

"Come on," the chief said. "Too hot to be outside. We make lunch, and then we take nap in cool hogan. Sound like good plan to you?"

"Uh, yeah." Running Bird followed him, still looking up at the eagle. "But how— OWW!" He tripped over a basketball-size rock that was embedded in the sun-baked soil, and in doing so, smacked his head into another one when he crashed to the ground.

Hearing the commotion, Rising Water hurried to his aid. "Running Bird! You okay?"

"Yeah, I think so," he groaned.

"Come on." The chief helped him up. "Let's get you inside."

38

Sitting by the campfire that night, Running Bird gazed up at the stars. "It sure is peaceful out here. I still can't get over how much the temperature drops after the sun goes down."

Rising Water didn't reply—he just stood up and walked away.

Deeming the chief's peculiar departure insignificant, Running Bird shrugged it off, and turned his attention back to the resplendent starlit sky.

About a minute later, he felt something flop down in his lap. Then he realized why the chief had stepped away—to retrieve him a blanket.

"How'd you know I was cold?"

"I just knew."

"Thank you."

"You welcome."

"Wow, this is beautiful." Running Bird held it up and admired its bright colors and striking geometric patterns. "Did you make this?"

"No, my wife did."

"You're married?"

"I was. Wife died couple years ago."

"Oh. I'm sorry." He continued to admire it. "Well, it's very pretty."

"Yes. She was master weaver. Very talented woman."

"How long did it take her to make it?"

"Blanket that size take about five hundred hours."

"Five hundred hours! You're kidding!"

"No. Serious. Weaving done on big upright looms. Take very long time."

"I had no idea. I figured it took a while, but I never imagined that it took *that* long." Running Bird covered himself with it, got comfortable, and gazed into the fire.

In no time, the dancing flames and crackling wood put him in such a state of surreal serenity, he began to feel as if he was dreaming. "Hey Chief," he murmured without looking away from the hypnotizing little inferno.

"Yes, Running Bird?"

"Earlier today, you said the eagle we saw was 'the most special thing in the world.' I know they're noble birds 'n all, but what did you mean by that? And how'd you teach it to do that trick with its wings, you know, when you held your arms out?"

"I never taught Liawatha anything."

"That's right. I forgot. You even gave it a name."

"No, Running Bird. I didn't give it a name either. You sit quiet, and I tell story. Storytelling very important to my people. It's how we pass down our history and values from one generation to the next.

"My wife, Liawatha, was amazing storyteller. She was sweet, wonderful woman. I love her very much. When she told stories, children would sit real still, and hang on her every word. Even me. I could listen to her tell same story a thousand times, and still never get tired of hearing it. And each night, after she finished telling stories to children in village, the children would get in line and wait for her to give them a big bear hug, before they go home.

"Those days, Running Bird," His voice fluttered. "Those days are the days I miss the most." The old man cleared his throat and wiped his eyes.

"The day after she died, my two-year-old nephew started hopping up and down, laughing and squealing with joy. He was so excited, we could hardly calm him down. All he kept doing was holding out his arms, smiling, and grunting. When we asked him what he doing, he pointed up to top of hoodoo and said, 'Look, Grandma on top of rock! Grandma wants big bear hug. Watch!' And when he reached out his little arms, eagle stretched her wings whole way out; hugged him back.

"Running Bird, I lived here all my life, and I never saw eagle land there before. Hoodoo is tall, but it's too close to hogan for eagles to land on. But not for Liawatha. She visit me every day since then. She sits on top of that rock, and I put my arms out; give her big bear hug. Then she puts out wings, and hugs me back. One day, I join her and we be together again. And I no have to miss her anymore."

"Wow," Running Bird gasped. "But how did your nephew know that was her up there? I mean, she looks like a regular eagle to me."

"Because animals and children can see things we cannot. You wait. You see her tomorrow. Normally, she show up after I get back from town."

"Town? You mean there's a town near here?"

"Yes. A small one." Rising Water stood up and stretched. "Come on. Getting late. We sleep now. Have big day tomorrow." He began walking toward the hogan.

"Yeah, I guess you're right. But what do we do about the fire?" Running Bird asked, looking at the waist-high blaze. "We can't just leave it burning."

Chief Rising Water turned around, straightened his arm, and whirled it around in a circular motion.

"Shoooop!" The flames disappeared right before Running Bird's eyes, as if they'd been sucked down into the earth.

"What fire?" the chief asked. "I see no fire. Come. We sleep now."

Running Bird stood there in the dim moonlight, gawking at nothing but ashes. "Don't you 'what fire?' me!" he exclaimed, spinning around toward Rising Water. "The fire we been sitting by all night! Where the hell did it go? And better yet, how did you do that?"!

"Ah, Running Bird," Rising Water said, wearing a smirk as he lay down in bed. "You sound like the children that Liawatha used to tell stories to. And I tell you the same thing she used to tell them: 'you only get one story per night,'" he said, pulling his sheets up.

39

Riding into town the following morning, Running Bird could hardly believe his eyes, for (with the exception of a few twenty-year-old automobiles), it appeared as if they'd stepped back into the late 1800's.

Main Street was nothing more than a wide stretch of dirt, where there existed almost as many horses and tumbleweeds as townspeople. Buildings constructed of old wooden planks lined both sides of the road. Even the entrance to the saloon sported a pair of old-fashioned, swinging slatted doors.

Running Bird drank in the surroundings. "This is like an Old West town. Why don't you live here? You know, in a regular house?"

"Too crowded," the chief replied.

"Too crowded? There can't be more than a couple hundred people who live here. How can you say it's too crowded?"

"Last count was 183. And that about 180 too many for me. I like living in hogan. Live traditional way. Others live modern way, like this. That fine for them, but not for me. I just like to visit.

I cash in gold at country store, shop at open air market, maybe sip a little firewater, and then head back."

"Sounds like a nice time. Where's the country store?"

"Up here. I show you."

Arriving at the country store, they tied Thunder and Lightning to the rail out front, and went inside.

"Hi, Rising Water," the shopkeeper said.

"Good morning, Harry," Rising Water replied.

"Harry?" Running Bird thought to himself, taken back by the man's contemporary name.

Then Harry greeted *him* by name. "And you must be Running Bird! Nice to finally meet you. How you feeling?"

Running Bird's mouth dropped open, but no words came out. He just stood there, looking dumbfounded.

Harry turned to the chief. "What's the matter with him? Ain't he got his voice back yet?"

"Yeah, it back. He fine." Rising Water nudged the stunned young man. "Running Bird. Tell Harry, 'hello.'"

"Hi. Um, have we met before?"

"No. What makes you ask that?"

"Because you called me 'Running Bird.' How'd you know my name?"

"How'd I know your name?"! Harry laughed. "Heck, you're all the chief's been talking about for the past two weeks!"

"Two weeks? That's impossible! He and I just met for the first time a couple days ago." Running Bird looked at Rising Water. "Didn't we?"

"Yeah, that's right."

Harry smiled. "Oh, you haven't told him yet."

"No, not yet."

"Haven't told me *what*?"

"I'll explain later," the chief replied, placing his gold on Harry's scale. "You go look around store. See if you need me buy you anything."

"Okay. But how—"

"You go now. Scoot! Baskets are over by door." He pointed to them. "And make sure you get some Mason jars and toilet paper too."

"Okay."

It didn't take long for Running Bird to realize Harry carried a wide variety of items, both traditional and modern, from household goods to hardware.

"Ah-ha, two ply." Running Bird spied the toilet paper. "And a toothbrush. And, let's see. What else?"

Several minutes later, Running Bird happened upon the aisle containing all of the Navajo-themed items. "Whoa!" he gasped, gazing at the vast selection: knives, awls, woven blankets, wool rugs, glass beads, seeds, silver jewelry, calumets, quivers, turquoise, colored sand, deer hides, venison, and gourds stretched into the distance as far as the eye could see. "Hey Chief, get over here! You gotta see this; they have *everything*!"

"I know what all Harry sells. Come on. Bring what you got up here so I can pay for it. We have more stops to make."

"Ahh-wight."

The chief looked at Harry. "What he say?"

But instead of replying, the shop owner burst out laughing.

"What so funny?"

Harry nodded to Running Bird.

Chief Rising Water turned around: his eyes became huge. For there stood Running Bird sporting a brand new pair of sunglasses with the price tag dangling by his nose, chewing on a piece of deer jerky; and his basket was so full, he had to use both hands to carry it. "Thunk!" He heaved everything up onto the counter.

The chief gawked at him for a moment. Then he looked at the basket. "Is, uh... the toilet paper under there, somewhere?"

"Yeah," Running Bird replied, the deer jerky still protruding from his mouth. "I got two-pwye!"

Wearing a blank look, Rising Water turned to Harry and murmured, "He say he got two-ply."

"Well then, I guess you're all set." Harry chuckled. "Will this be everything?"

"Yes, this *definitely* be everything!" Rising Water snatched his wallet from his pocket. "Can you keep this stuff behind counter? I pick it up later, after we get done in town. That okay?"

"Oh, sure. Anything for you, my friend."

"Thanks, Harry," Rising Water said, heading toward the door. "We be back in a little bit."

Running Bird yanked the price tag from his shades the second they stepped outside. "Thanks for buying me everything! I really love my sunglasses! Have you ever tried this jerky before? It's really good! It's so nice not having to squint anymore. Where are we goings next? I bet—"

"Woah." The chief held up his hand. "Slow up some. You bouncing around and talking so fast, people going to think you gone loco."

"Oh, sorry." He tried to calm himself down and walk normal. "So, where are we going now?"

"Livestock store."

"To the livestock store? You gonna buy a cow?"

"No."

"Another horse?"

"No."

"What then?"

"You see in a minute."

Up ahead, they entered a large building fornent a fenced in area containing cattle, horses, mules, and other domesticated animals.

"I know!" Running Bird said out of the blue. "We came here to buy horse feed for Thunder and Lightning!"

"No."

"No?"

"Nope." The chief walked up to the sales attendant. "Good morning, Miss Mary."

"Good morning, Chief," she replied. "And I bet you're Running Bird. Am I right? I am, aren't I? Well now, you're just as handsome as I imagined. Welcome to town."

"What the— Yes, ma'am, you're correct. But how do you know my name?"

"Rising Water told us, of course." She smiled, turning to the chief. "How many today? One or two?"

"Two, please."

"Two? Two what?" Running Bird watched the woman walk away. "And how do all these people know me?" He buried his face in his hands.

"What wrong?" The chief chuckled.

"I'm sho confoosed," he replied, his lips pressing against his palms.

The woman returned from the back. "There you are, Chief," setting something next to the register.

Running Bird spread apart his fingers and peeped through them, to see what she'd placed on the counter. "Rabbits! You're buying rabbits? They're not for us to eat, are they?"!

"No. Of course not."

"Good." He breathed a sigh of relief.

"They too tough. Meat all stringy. Gets caught between teeth."

"Ewww!" Running Bird's face contorted. "That's gross." He involuntarily shivered a little.

"Come on. Grab rabbits. We go now. Bye, Miss Mary. You have a nice day."

"You too, Chief. Nice to meet you, Running Bird."

On their way outside, Running Bird couldn't wait any longer; he began pestering the chief for answers before the store's doors even closed. "Okay, seriously! How do all these friggin' people know who I am?"!

"Because I am a shaman."

"What's a shaman?"

"Shaman is someone who can talk to spirit world. Can go into trance, and see things no one else can see. Can heal sick people, and give blessing to help have good hunting."

"That's uh, interesting," Running Bird replied, rubbing the side of his face in an up-and-down motion, wondering how to respond to such an absurd assertion. "So, you can talk to ghosts, huh? Hmmph. Well, I guess we better be going. Where do we—"

"You no believe me. That okay."

"That's not what I said. It's just that, well, you're a great guy 'n all, but you're bound to catch people a little off-guard when you tell them that you can talk to ghosts. Do you know what I mean?"

"Yes. I understand. Now let me ask you question: how you think I found you in desert?"

"I don't know. I guess you were just riding along and stumbled across me by accident or something."

"*By accident!*" Rising Water huffed. "Running Bird, people no go riding in desert for fun, any more than they jump in quicksand to swim! I *knew* you were out there. I saw you in a vision, just as clear as I see you now. Had vision long ago. Got ready for you and bought clothes for you from Harry's store *weeks* ago. He ask why I picking out stuff that's not my size. I tell him, 'Running Bird coming soon. Must get ready.' Told him about my dream; then he helped me pick out stuff for you. Miss Mary and a few other friends know too. They all very nice. Everyone is. You meet them soon. Not today though. Getting late. Come. Bring rabbits. We have one more stop to make."

40

"What's this place?" Running Bird asked.

"Hardware store," the chief replied. "They repair things."

"What all do they repair?"

"Pretty much anything."

"What did you bring for them to fix?"

"My phaeton."

"Your *what*?"

"My phaeton."

Just then, an elderly man emerged from the backroom. "Good morning, fellas. How ya doin'?"

"Hello, Ahiga," the chief replied. "We doing good. I need pick up my phaeton, so I figure I square up with you now, before I bring my girls over."

"Girls?"! Running Bird exclaimed, tugging on his shirtsleeve. "What girls?"!

"Stop." The chief smacked his hand away.

"Well, what girls are you talking about?"

Rising Water ignored him. "So, what do I owe you, Ahiga?"

"Aw, I don't know, Chief." He removed his old-time train engineer's cap and scratched his head. "How 'bout fifty bucks? That sound fair?"

"Yes. Sounds very fair. Here you go." Rising Water paid him.

"Thank ya, now." He shoved the wad of cash in his pocket without counting it. "It's around back. You can pick it up whenever you want."

"Alright, see you next time."

"Yup. Have a good one."

"Leave the rabbits here, Running Bird," the chief said, heading toward the exit. "We'll come back and get them in a minute."

"Okay, but what girls were you talking about back there?"!

"Thunder and Lighting. Why?"

"Thunder and— Oh, brother." He sighed.

When they returned to the hardware store with the horses, the chief asked Running Bird, "Can you go in and get rabbits, and meet me around back?"

"Sure." Running Bird hustled inside, retrieved the rabbits, and exited through the back door. "Wow!" He stopped in his tracks. "Is that your phaeton?"!

"Yes. You like it?"

"Yeah! A lot!" He ogled the elegant four-wheeled, horse-drawn carriage.

"Good. Here, give me rabbits." The chief took them from him, set them in the back, and hopped up onto the bench seat of the phaeton. "Come on. Climb up here. We need to pick up all the stuff that you picked out at Harry's store, yet."

"Okay, I— I'm com—" Running Bird couldn't take his eyes off the rabbits. "Hold on, Chief, that'll drive me crazy. I have to fix them."

"Fix them?"

"Yeah, just wait a minute," he replied, situating the two rabbit cages so that they sat side-by-side. Then he scooted each one forward and backward countless times, until the two square cages formed a perfect rectangle.

Finally, Rising Water wasn't able to tolerate his shenanigans any longer. "Running Bird! You've touched each one a thousand times! What you doing? Turn around and sit butt on seat, so we can go!"

"I'm sorry, but I was diagnosed as OCD when I was a kid. I can't help it."

"What is OBC?"

"No. O-C-D. It stands for 'obsessive-compulsive disorder.' It means that I need certain things to be situated symmetrically, or I go nuts inside. I remember when I was young, the doctor said—" Running Bird gasped. "I remember! I remember I have OCD! I don't remember anything else yet, but I remember *that*!"

"Ah, very good." The chief smiled. "See? No need to worry. Your memory will come back when it's ready, just like I said."

On their way out of town, the chief pulled back on the reins, stopping Thunder and Lightning in front of Harry's store. Running Bird ran in, grabbed their bags from behind the counter, and jumped back in the phaeton with everything.

"Ok, girls," Rising Water said, tossing the reins onto the floor. "Let's go home."

Running Bird looked down at the long leather straps lying by his feet. "Hey! Don't you need those to steer the horses?"

"No, they know the way. They very smart. Sometimes I lie down on bench seat and fall asleep on way home, and if I don't jump off as soon as we get home, they jerk carriage back and forth to wake me. Make me unhook them from phaeton, pronto! They have no patience."

"That's funny!"

"Wasn't very funny *one* time."

"Why? What happened?"

"Once they jerked so hard, they knock me off seat. Make me smack face on floorboard." He pressed his hand into his cheek, squishing his lips sideways.

Running Bird knew that he was being serious, but it was all he could do not to laugh. "That sucks," he replied, forcing a straight face.

Putting it out of his mind, Rising Water reached high into the air and leaned back. "Ahh, feels good to stretch. Keeps muscles loose and— Hey, look up there!"

Peering upward, Running Bird was rendered speechless. For there was Liawatha, larger than life, soaring through the sky as if she owned it. "Wow! Has she ever joined you on your way home from town before?"

"Yes. Lots of times. She knows routine, too."

Arriving back at the hogan, the chief gave Running Bird specific instructions: "I'll unhook phaeton from horses, and you take rabbits to garden. I join you in a minute. Then I show you what to do."

"Okay." Running Bird replied, lifting them out of the fancy carriage.

A couple minutes later, the chief met him at the vegetable patch. "Okay," he said. "You place your cage on ground next to mine, and—"

"Hey, look! Liawatha's perched atop her hoodoo. It looks like she's watching us."

"Yes. She is. Eagles have excellent eyesight. Now pay attention."

"Oh. Sorry."

"That okay. Now listen. On 'three,' we lift cage doors open. Ready?"

"Wait! No! *Not* ready! We're just going to turn them loose, after you paid good money for them?"

"Yeah, that's right."

"What do they do? Have a race?"

"Yeah, something like that. You ready?"

"It doesn't make much sense to me, but yeah, I guess so. Go ahead."

"Good. One. Two. Three!" They lifted the cage doors open, and the rabbits took off, hightailing it across the desert.

"Holy cow! Look how fast they can run! They can—" Just then, Liawatha swooped out of the sky and snatched up one of the rabbits.

"There she goes!" The chief cheered. "She happy now!"

Running Bird turned to Rising Water. "She's gonna eat the rabbit, isn't she?" he asked in an uneasy voice.

"Very difficult to live in desert. Very harsh climate. In Navajo tribe, it's the man's job to feed his family. And I will always honor that tradition. I will always make sure Liawatha have plenty to eat. Come. Getting too hot to be outside. Time for lunch."

41

"You okay over there?" Rising Water asked, casting his fishing line out into the river.

"Yeah," Running Bird replied. "Why do you ask?"

"Because you too quiet. When you this quiet, something on your mind. What you thinking about?"

Running Bird smirked. "You've gotten to know me pretty well, haven't you?"

"Yeah, well, we been around each other every day for several months now; it's only natural." The old man scooted closer to him, on the blanket they were sitting on. "Now tell me, what bothering you?"

"I was just thinking about my memory. Do you think I'll ever get it back?"

"Yes. Just no way of knowing when."

"Yeah, I suppose so." Running Bird fiddled with some pebbles by his feet. "I just figured that I would have it back by now. I'd like to know who I was— I mean, 'am.' Do you know what I mean?"

"Yes. Try not to worry. Your memory will come back when it's ready. Look out there." Rising Water nodded toward the horizon. "Sundown coming soon. No full moon, and no south wind. Means we about to catch really big fish. Go get more drinks and snacks from phaeton; we almost out. Then we enjoy beautiful sunset as we wait for fish to bite."

"Alright." Running Bird stood up. "Here. Watch my rod. I'll be right back."

The chief took it from him and placed it under his leg, to prevent a fish from pulling it into the river.

Feeling better after discussing his concerns, Running Bird trotted over to the phaeton and grabbed some refreshments.

As soon as he turned around to head back though, he noticed something up ahead in the distance, about twenty feet from their blanket.

He tried squinting, but he still couldn't make out what it was.

Then, all of a sudden, it lurched forward. Running Bird's eyes bulged from their sockets. It was a six-foot lizard, and it was headed right for his mentor. "Chief, run!" he yelled, breaking into a sprint. "Chief, look to your right! Get out of there!"

The predator closed in on its target.

Running Bird's heart pounded.

Just then, the chief raised his hand, signaling Running Bird to stop.

He was confused, but he obeyed.

Chief Rising Water didn't run away. For that matter, he never even got up. He just sat there as the venomous beast made its way onto their blanket, its foot-long tongue darting intermittently out of its mouth. Then it turned to the river and lowered its massive torso to the ground.

"It— it sat down beside him!" Running Bird gasped, his trepidation subsiding.

Then the chief placed his hand on its back and began talking to it.

Running Bird's eyes widened.

Shortly thereafter, the lizard lumbered away.

As soon as it departed, Running Bird raced over to Rising Water. "What was *that* all about?"!

"What you mean?"

"That prehistoric-looking lizard! What was that thing?"!

"A 'Gila monster.'"

"Oh my God! It even has the word 'monster' in its name?"!

"Yeah, that's right."

"Is that its *real* name?"

"Yes."

"Is it dangerous?"

"Yes." Rising Water stretched his neck out and raised his eyebrows, looking to see how far his line had washed downriver. "Gila monsters very dangerous. Very deadly. Kill several people every year."

"Kill sev— Weren't you afraid?"!

"No."

"No?"

"No."

"Why not?"

The chief looked Running Bird dead in the eye. "You really want to know why I not afraid of Gila monster?" he whispered.

Running Bird swallowed the lump in his throat. "Yeah." He held his breath.

"Because I got no *beef* with him," the chief replied, a devilish grin falling upon his face.

Running Bird's jaw dropped open. "Oh! You ought to be proud of yourself for that one!" He burst out laughing.

42

That night, out by the fire, Running Bird could not sit still. The chief looked at him and laughed. "What you doing? You act like you got ants in pants!"

"What do you mean? I'm not doing anything."

"Uh-huh. You up-down-up-down-up-down every two seconds. You walk over here to me, mess around with your fishing gear, and then go back to your seat. But you never do anything."

"Well, it sounds like we're in agreement then; I'm not *doing* anything." Running Bird returned to his seat, leaned back, and closed his eyes.

But not even a minute had passed, and he was already fidgeting with something else.

"*Now* what you playing with?"! Rising Water asked.

"A tiny gourd, Mr. Nosey! You're just getting irritated because you can't see what you're doing. You should come over here by the fire, if you want to organize your tackle box."

"I not Mr. Nosey," he mumbled.

"What?"

"No! I stay here! I fine." A few seconds elapsed, and he mumbled the remainder of his thought. "I no have eyes open, anyway; so light no help me, anyhow,"

"What did you say?"! Running Bird exclaimed, bolting to an upright position in his chair. "You don't have your eyes open?"!

"Now how you hear me say that?"

"Because you're a loud whisperer! Are your eyes open or not?"

"No. Eyes not open."

"So how do you see what you're doing, if your eyes are closed?"

"Through 'harmony.' Man with harmony sees with spirit, not eyes."

"Yeah, right." Running Bird snickered. "Uh-huh. Sure, I see."

"No. You don't." Rising Water looked over at the young man's fishing rod, which was lying perfectly parallel to his own— so he nudged it with his foot (*again*), knocking it askew. Then he sat back and waited.

Within seconds, Running Bird trudged over to where it was, to realign it.

The chief smirked. "See?"

"See *what*?"

"You over here a hundred times tonight because of your OCD thing. Like with rabbit cages in phaeton; you go cuckoo if our two fishing rods don't line up right."

"Do you mean to tell me that you've been messing with my stuff all night, just to make me come over here and fix it each time?"

"Yeah, that's right."

"But why?"!

"To teach you importance of having harmony. You trying to find *inner* peace, by trying to change what's going on *outside* yourself. That do no more good than chasing the wind.

"To find inner peace, Running Bird, you must look *inside* yourself." He touched his fingertip to the young man's chest. "You must look at the things you *can* change, not at the things you *can't*.

"Think of it this way: if you standing out in a storm, and you mad because you getting wet and cold, do you try to find peace by making clouds stop raining; or do you accept what's happening, and change what you are *able* to change—like by going indoors?"

"You go indoors."

"Yes. And right now, you feel like all your problems are raining down on you, and you're being tormented by the storms of life.

"Running Bird... problems are like raindrops. They will come throughout life no matter what; you can't stop them. It's how you choose to deal with them when they arrive, that will determine whether you ever find inner peace or not. See?"

Running Bird stood motionless, mesmerized by the old man's wisdom. "That makes sense."

Chief Rising Water smiled. "Good." He patted him on the shoulder. Then he returned his attention to his tackle box.

Running Bird retook his seat by the fire, contemplating his revelation as he watched Rising Water tinker with his sinkers and rubber worms. But something continued weighing on his mind. "Hey, Chief?"

"Yes?"

"Are you really doing all that rearranging with your eyes closed?"

"Yes. Come here. I show you."

Running Bird walked back over to him.

"Take off bandana and tie it around my eyes, like blindfold."

"Oh, okay! I see what you're doing. You want to prove it to me, huh?"

"Yes. Then you see what I talking about."

Running Bird tied his bandana around his mentor's eyes. Once he was sure he couldn't see anything, he returned to his seat.

But his doubt soon got the better of him, and he became obsessed by the chief's alleged ability to organize his tackle box, without being able to see.

"Man with harmony sees with spirit, huh?" Running Bird mumbled. "Well, see if you can see *this*!" he muttered, lobbing the little gourd that he was playing with earlier that night right at Rising Water's head.

Filled with indescribable anticipation, he watched the tiny fruit arc through the air on its way to its unsuspecting target.

But just then, his blindfolded teacher raised his hand up by his ear and *caught* the blessed thing.

Running Bird's eyes widened and his jaw dropped open.

"Nice try," the old man said, "but you have to do better than that."

43

"You, and your gold!" Harry chuckled, shaking his head. "Seems like you've found a never-ending supply of it out there somewhere."

"Nah, that impossible." The chief watched him weigh his latest findings.

"So, where's your partner in crime?"

"Who? Running Bird?"

"Yeah."

"He outside talking to Miss Mary."

"That poor woman. She sure is worried about tonight, isn't she?"

"What happening tonight?"

"Oh, she didn't tell you about the chantway?"

"No, I haven't talked to her yet. Who is chantway for, Harry? Who's sick?"

"Her niece, Nihanna."

"Nihanna? She only a child! What happened? What wrong with her?"!

"Now, Chief, calm down. There's nothing you can do."

"Who performing ceremony? I do it! Who—"

"Chief! Be quiet and listen. Miss Mary already asked Shaman Brave Wolf to perform it."

"Shaman Brave Wolf?"!

"Yes. So Nihanna is in very good hands. The chantway begins tonight at 8 pm. Can you make it?"

Rising Water said nothing. He just stood there, glaring at his friend for asking such a stupid question.

"Okay then." Harry tinkered with the knickknacks on the counter, trying to escape the sting of the chief's piercing stare. "I guess I'll see you tonight."

"Yes. You will. Running Bird and I both be there." He stomped out of the store, colliding with Running Bird in the doorway.

"Whoa! Hey, Chief. I was just on my way in to meet you. Are you done already?"

"Yes!" he replied, parading right past him.

"Hold on, Chief! Wait! What's wrong?"

"We go now!"

"We're leaving town already? But we never leave this early. Why are we—"

"Have lots to do today."

"We do? Like what?" Running Bird asked, climbing atop Thunder.

"Have to get ready for tonight."

"Tonight? Oh, do you mean the chantway ceremony?"

"Yes. Where Miss Mary?"

"She's gone."

"Gone where?"

"I don't know. She explained what a chantway ceremony is and started to tell me about tonight, but then someone called her, and she had to go. Are you alright?"

"I fine," he grumbled, spurring Lightning.

Several minutes into their trip, Running Bird peered over at Rising Water. Maybe it was due to how the sun was striking his face, or maybe it was because he was distressed, but he looked especially aged all of a sudden. The creases in his weathered skin were deeper and more defined than usual. And his demeanor carried with it a disturbing aura of desperation.

They rode the whole way home without speaking. Running Bird had never seen him act this way before.

Unsure of what to do, and unaccustomed to being home from town so early, he decided to lie down for a while, to give Rising Water a chance to cool off.

But he couldn't get him off his mind. After a half hour of tossing and turning, Running Bird got up, walked over to the doorway, and peered outside.

Just as he suspected, the chief was sitting about ten yards away with his back toward him, facing the magnificent sunrise, meditating.

Wondered what was on his mentor's mind, Running Bird folded his arms and leaned against the doorjamb.

Rising Water sensed the young man's eyes upon him. Without ever turning around, he invited his pupil to join him. "Come, Running Bird," he said, patting the ground with his palm, sending tiny clouds of dust up into the air. "Sit."

He walked over to Rising Water and sat down.

"Running Bird." The chief began speaking in a somber voice, still looking off into the distance. "I just want to say 'thank you.'"

"Me? You want to thank *me*?"

"Yes." He nodded. "Do you know why we were brought together?"

Running Bird thought for a moment. "So you could save my life?"

"Ah, you still only see small picture. I tell you the truth: to see big picture, you must *shut* eyes. We were brought together, not just because you needed me, but because I needed you, too.

"Nothing in life happens by accident. And sometimes, I forget that. Our paths were destined to cross since the beginning of time, before First Man and First Woman ever walked the land. And everything in life—both good and bad—happens for a reason: to keep harmony and balance in universe."

Running Bird ogled the horizon as he drank in the chief's words of wisdom.

"You see," Rising Water continued, "when a man fights with another man, there will be one winner. And there will be one loser. And everything stays in balance.

"But when a man fights with himself, there can be no winner. Inner self is disturbed and falls away, causing same kind of disharmony as if sun suddenly fell away from center of solar system. But what I learn from you keeps me from fighting with myself."

"You've learned stuff from *me*?"

"Yes. You show me many things. Many important things."

Silence ensued. Running Bird tried to recall what he could have ever taught his teacher, but he couldn't think of anything. "Chief?"

"Yes, Running Bird?"

"Will I ever be as smart as you? Or be able to do cool stuff like you can do?"

"What cool stuff?"

"You know, like a few minutes ago... how did you know I was watching you from the doorway? And how did you heal my throat? And how do you talk to spirits? I just don't see—"

"SCREEEELLL!" Liawatha hollered down to them from atop her favorite hoodoo.

"Dag-nabbit, that woman! And see? Like that, right there! How the heck do you communicate with animals? Nothing happens when I look at her and hold *my* arms out!" Running Bird yelled, looking up at her, extending his arms out from his sides.

Suddenly—against his will—he froze in place. He tried to look away from the noble creature, but he couldn't.

Finally, after several long seconds, his body collapsed to the ground as if he'd been hanging from a rope that had been cut.

Chief Rising Water emitted a little chuckle. "You okay, Running Bird?"

"Yeah. I think so." He moaned, grimacing as he pushed himself up to a seated position. "What happened?"

"*Now*, do you see big picture of why we were brought together? You ask me if you will ever be able to do the things I can do." Rising Water turned and looked at him. "But you can *already* do them."

"Buh how?" Running Bird asked, holding out his tongue, wiping it clean of the dirt and sand that entered his mouth when he fell. "Thah duthn't make thenth."

"Sure it does. You have special ability that only handful of people in whole world have; you just didn't know it till now.

"Think of it this way: it's like a treasure that you have inside you that is locked inside a hidden chest. And you just found the chest. Now the question is, can you find the key that opens it?"

"Sounds a lot like my memory. That's locked up inside me somewhere too, and I can't get to that either."

"Yes. But one day, you will not just get memory back, but you will receive much more, if you just keep doing what's right. Do your best to live in harmony. Practice meditation. Learn how to become 'one' with all that surrounds you, and then you will find key that opens chest. *And* get your memory back.

"But right now, we need to start getting ready for chantway ceremony. We have lots to do. Must be well rested and spiritually strong to support Shaman Brave Wolf tonight."

44

rriving at Miss Mary's mobile home, Running Bird and Rising Water dismounted Thunder and Lightning, and walked toward the crowd.

Running Bird looked at the hodgepodge of horses and automobiles. "Geesh, I never would have guessed this many people around here owned cars. Some of them are expensive, too."

"You must remember that we Indians have wide range of lifestyles, nowadays," the chief replied. "Some live in hogans, and they fish, hunt, and grow own food like us. Others go on to college, get modern job, and buy a house. Everybody different."

"Holy cow, look over there!" Running Bird pointed at a limousine. "Who do you think came here in that?"!

"Probably Shaman Brave Wolf."

"Is he rich?"

"Yes. He very wealthy."

"What's he do for a living?"

"He owns a casino."

Running Bird stopped in his tracks. "He what?"

"Well, he doesn't own whole thing, but he owns a big part of it. It not that big of deal. Not all that uncommon either. More Indians involved in casinos than you think."

"I don't understand. How?"

"Big business come out to Indians who own large territory. They make deal to use land—to build big casino on it—and make Indian part owner of business in exchange for land. Everybody make lots of money. Bring many jobs to areas where many people are desperate for work.

"But many traditional Indians against modernization. They say we don't need casinos to survive. I suppose both sides have good argument, but I old man now. So I just keep to myself. Stay out of everyone's way. My days of fighting are over, Running Bird. I too old and tired to fight. I just turn head and look other way now... like in *that* direction!" He perked up, nodding at the huge feast that just came into view.

Sashaying over to the buffet, Rising Water and Running Bird loaded two plates full of food, and partook in delightful conversation as they mingled among the guests.

"This is a lot different than old-fashioned chantway ceremonies, isn't it?" Running Bird asked.

"Yes, very different. But it will serve same purpose. Look, here come Shaman Brave Wolf."

"Hello, Rising Water." He greeted him. "How you doing this evening?"

"I fine. How are you? You all ready for later?"

"Yes. Very ready. This is a nice, unexpected surprise. I didn't think I would have such an opportunity in this lifetime. I'm very honored. But at the same time, I'm sorry you weren't the one chosen, Rising Water." Shaman Brave Wolf placed his hand on the chief's shoulder.

"Thank you for kind words, but you deserve it. You a good man. Like I told Running Bird earlier, we must remain at peace with self, even when things in life do not go the way we want. Must be okay not with not understanding, and not knowing answers to everything all the time. It just wasn't my turn to lead ceremony tonight—was your turn. And I happy for you. I very honored to be your friend for so long, and I will miss you very much."

Shaman Brave Wolf smiled and embraced him. "You take care of this man, Running Bird. And make sure you listen to him. He's a very wise man."

"Yes, sir. I most definitely will."

"Very well then. I'll go finish making my rounds. Then we'll go inside and perform the ceremony."

Rising Water looked on as his fellow shaman disappeared into the crowd. "Brave Wolf is very lucky man, Running Bird. He always at peace. Always happy and smiling."

"Of course he's always happy; he's rich!"

"Nah! Running Bird! You know better than that. You know material things not the reason for a wise man's happiness."

"You're right." Running bowed his head. "I don't know what I was thinking."

"Ah, that's okay. That why we have each other: to keep each other on the right path." He rested his arm atop Running Bird's shoulders. "Man must remember he is like little boy on bicycle, who just learned to ride without training wheels. He must not ever think he too big for help. And he should not shun, but rather welcome the helping hand of another man who is willing to run alongside him."

"Thanks, Chief. Thanks for helping me, you know, to stay on course and everything."

"Ah, my pleasure, Running Bird. My pleasure indeed! Now follow me. Many people here. Many you never met before. I introduce you."

"Sounds good."

"And if we plan our route right, we be smart and end up back over at food just about the time we have room in stomachs to enjoy seconds!"

"Wow, you *are* wise!"

"Thank you. Let's start over there." The chief gestured toward the back of the group.

Ambling to the rear of the gathering, neither of them could help but to notice Brave Wolf's frolicky behavior.

"I sure hope I'm that happy-go-lucky when I'm his age," Running Bird said.

"Yes, he normally outgoing, but he definitely extra happy tonight." The chief chortled.

"Why? Because of the ceremony?"

"Yes. First, he will receive great honor for healing Nihanna. Then he gets to finally go home."

"Finally go home? Uh... yeah, okay." All of the sudden, Running Bird noticed the size of Miss Mary's residence. "Say, Chief, how are all these people going to fit in that tiny trailer?"

"They can't. Only ones allowed inside are shamans, and Nihanna's immediate family. Nihanna not been able to get out of bed for over a week. Must hurry and perform ceremony tonight, or she may not make it."

Just then, Shaman Brave Wolf appeared in the doorway of the trailer with Nihanna's mother, Johona. He announced that the ceremony was about to begin, and then dashed inside.

"Come, Running Bird!" Chief Rising Water said. "We must hurry!"

"What? Who, me? But you said that only shamans and family members are allowed to go inside!"

"Yeah, that's right!" The chief grabbed his hand. "Now come on!" He pulled him through the crowd.

The half dozen individuals who were permitted inside made their way to Nihanna's bedroom, where she lay unconscious.

Running Bird could hardly believe how feeble and helpless the child appeared.

Shaman Brave Wolf nodded to those present, letting them know that the time had come to summon every bit of energy they had, and to join him in prayer.

Reminiscent of when the chief healed Running Bird's throat, Shaman Brave Wolf closed his eyes, inhaled a deep breath, and raised his arms out from his sides.

Then he thrust his hands forward and slammed them together, where they began to shake and glow, just as Running Bird had anticipated.

Outside, everyone held hands, and formed a huge circle around the trailer and held hands.

The wind swirled and whipped about, and flashes of lightning filled the sky.

When the radiating sphere of energy between the shaman's palms reached its peak, his eyes shot open, and he plunged his hands down onto the child's chest, sending the luminous orb into her diseased body.

The little girl's back arched high off the bed, her eyes sprang open, and her lungs filled with air.

At the same time, the shaman's eyes closed, his muscles went limp, and his body collapsed to the floor.

Nihanna looked around her room, searching for a familiar face. And then she spied one. "Mommy!" She held out her arms.

"Nihanna!" Johona raced to her side. Weeping with joy, she lifted her up and held her tight.

Squirming around, the now-healthy child peered out from under her mother's long hair, at everyone in her room. Then she leaned back and looked Johona in the eye. "Mommy?"

"Yes, honey?"

"If all these people are here for a sleepover, I think we're gonna need a bigger bed."

45

On the way home from the chantway ceremony, the chief rubbed his stomach and smiled. "Oh my, I full!"

Running Bird remained quiet.

"I really like Miss Mary's potato salad. I think that my favorite."

Still, Running Bird said nothing.

"Do you like her potato salad, Running Bird?"

"Uh-huh," he muttered.

"Ah, me too! Her iced tea also plenty good, but sometimes I think she need more sugar in it. Southern tea famous for being sweet. That how I—"

"Honestly, Chief! Tea? Potato salad and tea? *That* is what's on your mind right now? How can you be so heartless and unfeeling?"!

"Heartless? I not heartless. What wrong, Running Bird? Are you mad at me?"

"Yes! I mean, no. I— I just don't understand!"

"What don't you understand? Tell me."

"I'm trying to figure out what happened at the ceremony. I understand how Nihanna was healed; that, I get. But what about Shaman Brave Wolf?"

"What about him?"

Running Bird looked at Rising Water, his eyes bursting wide open. "Chief, the man dropped dead right in front of us, and no one even flinched! Dead, Chief! And I'm just a little freaked out about it right now! I mean, did you know that was going to happen? You told me that he was going *home* afterwards. But he didn't! He friggin' died! Why did you lie to me?"!

The chief pulled Lightning's reins in, stopping her, causing Running Bird to ride up ahead without him.

When Running Bird noticed he was alone, he turned Thunder around and rode back. "You okay?"

But this time, it was the chief who refused to respond.

"I'm sorry, Chief. I didn't mean to explode. I just—"

"Get off horse!"

"Get— get down?"

"Yes!"

Both of them dismounted.

Rising Water tromped over to Running Bird, his nose within inches of his student's. "Chief Rising Water is good, honorable man. And honorable men don't lie!"

"I'm sorry." Running Bird bowed his head. "I didn't mean to offend you. Is— is that what was supposed to have happened?"

"Yes."

"But you said he was going home after the ceremony."

"Right. And he did. He healed Nihanna, and then he went home. Now he with family. He very lucky man. I don't—"

"Wait! He *did* go home?"

"Yes. Of course."

"So, when you said 'home,' you meant the *spirit* world."

"Yeah, that's right."

"And he's been apart from his family... because they're all deceased."

"Yes. And now he gets to be with them."

"I understand." He sighed and turned around, his head hanging low.

"Running Bird. Hold on. Turn back around and look at me, please. You say you understand, but you still look sad. Why?"

"Because the man is dead, Chief. I just can't believe—" Running Bird clenched his jaw and turned away, his eyes welling up with tears.

"*What* can't you believe? It's okay. You can tell me."

"I just can't believe he's gone. Shaman Brave Wolf. He's just... *gone*. I never took time to think about it before. You know, about 'life.' It's just so fragile. And precious. And up until an hour ago, I've always taken it for granted. Just like pretty much everyone does, I guess. I mean, we could literally be here one day, and gone the next." Running Bird looked down at the ground, giving the sand a light kick. "I guess I'll be 'gone' one day too, huh? Just like Brave Wolf."

"But Running Bird, he *not gone*."

"What do you mean, 'he's not gone'?"

"He not gone; he just went home. Think of it like, he just moved to a different place, that's all; he not gone any more than you and I are gone."

Seeing the young man trying to make sense of what he was articulating—but grasping absolutely nothing—Rising Water tried explaining it a different way. "Running Bird, the problem is that you still using only your eyes to see. Do this: think of Miss Mary's house. Picture it in your mind, okay?"

"Okay."

"Now tell me, what's the difference between a house, and a person's home?"

"A house and a home are the same thing. There're synonyms."

"No. Not same thing! Forget syn— synothings! And forget about everything else you think you know! Now, what makes Miss Mary's home unlike any other home in the world?"

"Because that one is hers. She lives in that one."

"That's right. Because she lives in that one. And what happens to it if she moves someplace else?"

"Nothing. It just sits there."

"You right again. So, is it still her home?"

"No."

"Exactly. But the outside will look the same: it will still have siding, roof, and doors, but no Miss Mary inside. She just moved someplace else. Now, look at me and tell me what you see."

Having only the light of the moon to assist him, Running Bird squinted. "I see your jewelry and—"

"No! Turn around!" The chief grasped Running Bird's shoulders and spun him about. "Forget about your eyes! Look out there somewhere!" He pointed to the distant horizon. "Now, with your *heart*, look at me and tell me what you see."

"Um, I see the fun stuff we do, like panning for gold and fishing. And how you take care of me. And how we ride horses together, and go into town, and—"

"Good. Now face me again."

As soon as Running Bird turned around, the chief jerked open the top of his shirt, revealing his aged body. "Now, using your eyes like you always want to do, tell me what you see."

"I see your grey chest hair."

"Right. What else you see?"

"You mean your skin?"

A big smile made its way onto the chief's face. "That's right," he whispered. "Nothing but *skin*. Running Bird, snakes in grass have skin. Potatoes in ground have skin. Skin and hair are nothing. They are like siding and roof are, to house.

"You see, when our spirits leave our bodies, they don't cease to exist; they just go from this world, to the spirit world, leaving our skin and hair behind. And if you live the good way while on earth, you live for forever in spirit world.

"Yes, I will miss my friend, Brave Wolf. But right now, he is laughing with his wife and parents. He is more happy now than he ever imagined he could be. And that makes me happy for him.

"I will see him again one day, and then I live forever with him, Liawatha, and everyone else who died before me. So, no need to be sad.

"Look, if you still around when my spirit passes on to spirit world, it okay if you miss me; but please, don't be sad. Just imagine me finally being with my wife again, and think of how happy I will be. And then I want you to smile, and be happy for me. Okay?"

"Okay, I will."

"You promise?"

"Yes. I promise."

"Thank you. And since we talking about all this right now, I have one more very important thing to tell you. You listen now. Do you remember the first time you saw Liawatha?"

"Yes."

"You were looking up in air at her instead of where you were walking, and you tripped over a little rock, and hit head on a big rock. And then I needed to help you back into hogan, and doctor you up all over again."

"Yeah." Running Bird rolled his eyes. "How could I forget *that*?"

"Good. Do you remember the *exact* rock you tripped over?"

"Yes. I remember."

"Good. Now you listen. On the eastern side of that rock, right next to it, sand is only few inches deep. Under sand are some boards. And under boards are things I want you to have after my spirit passes to spirit world. When that day comes, you dig in that spot. Whatever you find there belongs to you. You promise now."

"Yes, Chief. I promise. I will."

"Good!" He smiled and put his arm atop the young man's shoulders. "Now let's get back to hogan. It getting cold out here."

46

The first thing Rising Water noticed when he awoke the following morning was that Running Bird's bed was empty. "Now what that boy up to? He never get up this early."

Making his way outside, the chief looked around, but Running Bird was nowhere to be found. Rubbing the sleep out of his eyes, he walked around back.

There, he found Running Bird sitting on the ground with his legs crossed, facing the sunrise with his eyes closed, meditating.

Relishing in his pupil's progress over the past two years, Rising Water grabbed a basket from his wickiup and proceeded to his garden. He tried to concentrate on his vegetables, but his student was proving to be a huge distraction. Although he'd seen Running Bird meditate many times before, this time, something was very different. And the fact that he couldn't put his finger on it was driving him nuts.

Just then, the contents of his basket caught his eye. "Ugh!" he griped, seeing that he'd been picking vegetables that were nowhere near ripe. "That 'nuff of this!" The old man snatched a green tomato out of his basket, grinned like an ornery adolescent, and threw it at Running Bird.

Rising Water watched it arc through the air, his eyes sparkling with anticipation. Like a bowler trying to steer his ball down the lane, he shifted his hips, leaned to the right, and raised a shoulder in a valiant effort to keep the tiny projectile on track.

Just as he was about to burst forth with triumphant laughter, Running Bird drew his elbow in at the very last second, allowing the tomato to sail right past him.

"Humph!" The chief stewed over it for a moment. Then he grabbed another tomato from his basket, raised it to his cheek, and took aim. "Ha!" He sent it soaring toward his protégé.

Rising Water could barely contain himself as he watched it continue on a perfect path.

But just before it struck him, Running Bird tilted his head to the side, permitting it to whiz by, just like the first one did.

The chief's mouth dropped open in utter disbelief. And then he heard his own words come back to haunt him: "Nice try!" Running Bird laughed. "But you'll have to do better than that."

"Oh, you think you funny guy!" The chief tromped over to him.

"No." He looked up at his mentor, his face radiating with unprecedented confidence. "I can do it now. You know, like you can."

The chief furrowed his brow. "What can you do like me?"

"I had a vision last night. Everything you've been trying to teach me suddenly became clear. I understand. And I can see things the way you do, too, without using my eyes."

"That's wonderful, Running Bird! That's great news. But seeing without eyes is only small part of picture. Learning to live harmoniously in universe going to take very long time. Having a vision about me throwing tomatoes at you is a nice start, but some people *never* able to become one with nature. You must still be very patient. Okay?"

"But chief, my vision wasn't about you throwing vegetables at me."

"No?"

"No. Spirits came to me last night. They told me to come out here before sunrise and wait on Jasper to visit. They said that if I had faith, I would be blessed with wisdom and special talents. So I came out here to meditate. Jasper visited. And now I—"

"Wait. Who is Jasper?"

Running Bird looked down at his lap. "All right, Jasper, I have to be going, so you have to leave now."

Chief Rising Water watched in awe as a huge copperhead snake slithered out of Running Bird's lap, where it had been camouflaged by all the fringes on his pants. "How you do that? People try to become one with universe their whole life! And most *never* do! Yet *you* can do, after having only one vision?"!

"Yeah, that's right." Running Bird rose to his feet, swiping dirt from his pants. "I mean, it's not like Jasper walked up and talked to me, but we were able to communicate—you know, like 'read each other's minds.' Anyways, are you hungry? I sure am. How about I fix us some breakfast?" Running Bird headed back.

But the chief remained still. "This make no sense." He just stood there, gawking at the reptile slithering away. "It just not possible. It—"

"Chief!" Running Bird called to him. "I thought you were following me. Is everything okay?"

"Uh, yeah Running Bird. I fine... I guess," he replied, scratching his head.

47

"Even the rabbits think you're batty," Running Bird said, watching them sniff the items in the back of the phaeton, on their way back from town.

"I not batty." Rising Water huffed. "Everything I buy from Harry this morning, very important."

Running Bird turned around and faced forward. "Pfft, yeah right! Feathers, leather, more Mason jars, sand verbenas, sticks... Seriously, Chief, who buys stuff like this, except you?"

"You no like sand verbenas?"

"Well, yeah. They're pretty, but—"

"I like, too." He smiled. "Smell them. They one of very few flowers that grow good in desert. When I was little boy, my mother used to plant them around hogan. Make place look very nice. Very nice indeed."

"That sounds good, but what about everything else?"

"Everything else is for tonight."

"Tonight? I didn't know we had to go out tonight."

"We don't," the chief replied, parking the phaeton by the hogan. "We not going anywhere. I been saving tonight for a surprise. Had to wait for full moon to come. And tonight, we have one. Come on, let's get everything unloaded."

"All right. If you say so." Suddenly, Running Bird felt another pair of eyes upon him. Scanning the area, he quickly located the culprit and smiled. "Hey chief, look up."

"At what?" He tilted his head back. "Oh! Liawatha! She sees her rabbits. She must be hungry. I'll put stuff in hogan and give horses water. You take rabbits to garden and cut them loose for Liawatha. And then we meet inside, and get ready for tonight. Going to be a fun day, today."

"Okay. Sounds like a—" Running Bird stopped in his tracks. "Did you just say we're going to have *fun* today?"

"Yes!" The chief threw his hands in the air as he walked away. "Big fun. We have really big fun today."

"Big fun, huh?" Running Bird murmured, raising his eyebrows. "Now *there* is something I never thought I'd hear him say."

48

"Okay, I sit here, and you sit there," Rising Water said. "That way, we both be able to reach big pile of supplies."

"I feel like a kid getting ready to have an 'arts 'n crafts' class." Running Bird chortled.

"Ah, not quite. This not for kids. Only for men. First thing we do is root through handles."

"Handles? What handles?"

"These." The chief held one up.

"Oh, the sticks! Gotcha!" Running Bird inspected a few of them. "When you say, 'root through the sticks,' what—"

"Not sticks. Handles."

"—root through the *handles*, what am I supposed to be looking for?"

"Look for one that feels good in hand. Good, straight, strong one. Not too thick. And not too thin. Or it will be hard to hold and swing around."

"Swing around? Maybe I should have asked first, 'what kind of handle is this?' I mean, a handle to what?"

"Decorative club."

"You mean, like a tomahawk?"

"No. A tomahawk has long handle and is used like modern day axe. Decorated club very different. Has short handle like war club, but is used only in ceremonies."

"Oh, I get it now! That's why all the handles are shaped like 'Y's'—so we can attach one of those round stones between the two prongs at the top. Then we can decorate it however we want, with the feathers and all, right?"

"Yes." He nodded. "You right. Today is a very important day: the day an Indian makes his first decorative club is a rite of passage, Running Bird. So take your time. How you decorate your club tells much about you, your values, and what's in your soul.

"I never forget the day my father sat down with me and helped me make mine. And now, today, I have honor of helping *you*. And this day, too, I will never forget. I will always hold it close to my heart."

Running Bird stopped examining the handle he was holding and looked up. The chief's face couldn't have been any closer. Looking into the old man's eyes, Running Bird suddenly had a revelation: in all the time that they'd spent together, Rising Water never mentioned anything about having *children of his own*.

He'd discussed his wife, plenty. He'd even showed him pictures of her, and doted over his favorite one—the one of them kissing on their wedding day. But he never showed him any pictures of his children... because he didn't have any.

Swallowing the lump in his throat, Running Bird responded, "This is one day that I, too, will never forget."

A moment of silence ensued, and both men's eyes welled up with tears.

"Ah, very good!" The chief popped up from his seated position, shielding his face from Running Bird. "I go— hu-umm." He cleared his throat, "—go get us drink of water. Hot in here!"

Like sneaky little kids, they both wiped their eyes and composed themselves while they were apart, and when the chief returned, they recommenced the construction of their decorative clubs.

"Kunk, kunk, kunk, kunk." The chief beat two rocks into each other.

Running Bird looked at him. "What are you doing?"

"Using hunk of granite to shape head of club," he replied, wiping sweat from his brow. "Granite much harder than sandstone. Make head of club look perfect for ceremony. You need granite to shape yours?"

Holding the head of his club about two inches from his nose, Running Bird scrutinized it. "No, I must have gotten lucky. I like the way mine looks, just the way it is. Look at the symmetrical pattern that I'm painting on the side." He held it out for Rising Water to see.

The chief inspected it. "Ah, Running Bird, that's very good work. Very detailed. Shows strong morals. Everyone who sees this will know that this was made by a man of great honor. Nice job, Running Bird. Yes, very nice job indeed."

Awestruck by his mentor's high praise, Running Bird sat motionless, marveling at his fine craftsmanship. Every so often, he'd rotate his piece of handiwork, to check it out from a different angle.

Meanwhile, the chief continued sculpting the head of his club. "Kunk, kunk, kunk... kunk, kunk, OWWW!"

Running Bird never even flinched. "Whatja do?" he mumbled.

"Hit thumb! Smash-eee it really bad!" The chief squeezed his eyes shut, clutching his injury with his opposite hand.

Glancing over at him, Running Bird noticed that he was making weird faces—as if something was wrong. "Huh? Whatja say you did?"

"Smashed thumb!" He popped it in his mouth, trying to alleviate the pain.

"Humph," Running Bird replied, his eyes remaining locked on his club. "Does it hurt?"

"DUTH EH HERT? YEAH, EH HURZH?"! The chief yelled, his thumb still in his mouth.

"Well you don't have to shout!" Running Bird snapped out of his trance. "Hold it over here. Let me see."

The chief thrust his throbbing digit right in front of his pupil's eyeballs.

Running Bird looked at it; the man's fingernail had already turned purple. "That sucks," he said, returning his attention to his club.

"Yeah, I say so sucks!" The chief's eyes widened.

49

Dressed in ornate Navajo Indian regalia, Rising Water finished assisting Running Bird with the application of his face paint just as the sun sank behind the horizon. "Ah-ha, perfect," he said, taking a few steps back to get a better look at his protégé. "You look good, Running Bird. You look very good. How you feel?"

Standing in the mysterious field of energy radiating from the campfire, Running Bird held up his decorated club and smiled. "I feel spiffy," he said, his smile suddenly disappearing.

"Ah! I agree!" The chief replied, noticing the change in his student's expression. "Running Bird, what wrong? Why you look so serious all of a sudden?"

"Nothing's wrong. I just felt weird for a second, that's all."

"You sick?"

"No. I'm fine. Something just kind of tingled behind my eyes when I answered you just now."

Rising Water thought for a second, trying to recall what he'd said. "All I asked you was, 'How you feel?'"

"Right. And I said... 'spiffy.' I don't know. It's nothing, I guess. Anyway, I feel fine now. So, what's next?"

"Meditation. We sit next to each other, give thanks for our health and happiness, and humbly ask for help to make your induction ceremony go good."

"Wait! Whose induction ceremony? Mine?"!

"Yes. Tonight, Running Bird, you become real shaman—I thought you knew."

"No, I sure didn't know *that*! I can't believe it! I'm going to be a shaman? A real shaman, just like you?"!

"Yes. Just like me."

"Are you sure I'm ready?"

"Yes. Very sure. Now relax. Clear mind and meditate. Then we play the drums my father made when I was a boy. You remember how I showed you different ways of playing for different kinds of dances, right?"

"Yes, I remember."

"Good." The chief touched fire to the end of his calumet and took a few puffs.

"What are you smoking?" Running Bird asked.

"Dry leaves of tobacco. Here." He handed him the long-stemmed ceremonial pipe.

Running Bird placed it to his lips and inhaled. The flavor of the raw plant left much to be desired, but he knew it must be very important to the ritual, so he partook in the requirement a few more times—until he began to feel nauseated. "Blaaach!" He squinched his face up and gave it back.

Then he noticed Rising Water chewing on something. "What's that stuff? Gum?"

"No. Dried cactus buttons. Here." He put several in his hand.

Before putting them in his mouth, Running Bird held them under his nose and sniffed. "They don't smell like anything."

"No, no smell," the chief added, crossing his legs as he prepared to meditate.

Figuring they had no taste if they had no odor, Running Bird tossed them atop his tongue and commenced chomping.

Pulling his left heel into his crotch, he, too, prepared to meditate. Bending forward, he reached for his other foot, but in the midst of doing so, he froze. His eyes burst wide open. Then he squeezed them shut, and his face morphed into an expression that screamed, "Oh my God, I'm gonna puke!"

Rendered speechless by the bitter slime that was now oozing from the abominable little objects in his mouth, he feverishly mimed his all-important message. But the chief didn't understand.

"They're... heh-gluuch!" Running Bird tried to communicate the reason for his consternation but gagged instead.

With his arms and hands still flailing from his futile miming attempt, he tried to vocalize his dilemma once more.

"They're... HEH-GLUUCH!!" He experienced a full-blown dry heave that time.

Seeing that he was experiencing some kind of problem, the chief assisted him in the clarification of his issue by asking one simple question: "Bitter, huh?"

"Mmm-hmmm!" Running Bird vigorously shook his head up and down.

Rising Water chuckled. "Here. Wash down with this." He handed him some water.

Running Bird guzzled every last drop.

Shivers rumbled through his body, and his jaw involuntarily quivered, remnants of his beverage dripping from his chin.

Realizing he had to collect his thoughts and focus, he sat erect, took one last deep breath, and tried to put the vile event out of his mind.

After meditating for a while, Rising Water slid a drum over to him. Then he rose to his feet and advanced toward the fire in a slow, methodical manner, almost like he was requesting its permission to approach.

Remaining seated, Running Bird tapped the drum's taut deerskin surface, sparking the chief's right foot to scooch back and forth on the ground.

Then his left foot lunged forward, mimicking the action of its mate.

As Running Bird's confidence grew, and the rhythm of his drumming became more dynamic, it acted like a magical elixir, injecting immense power and purpose into the chief's performance.

Round and round, Shaman Rising Water circled the flames as Running Bird played on—until one time—he did not emerge from behind the fire, alone; he was accompanied by two fellow Navajo Indian warriors, who were dancing alongside him.

Untroubled the unexpected guests, Running Bird gazed up at the spectacular sky. "Wow!" he gasped, for the stars were not their usual pinpoint size; they were as big as hot air balloons. "Hold still." He raised his hand up to the closest one, hoping to grab ahold of it. But it was just out of reach.

Forced to be content with ogling it, as opposed to capturing it, he turned his attention to the man sitting next to him, who happened to be playing the other drum. It was Shaman Brave Wolf. "Hi," Running Bird said, bringing his knees up to his chest, clasping his hands together in front of his shins.

As Shaman Brave Wolf played the drum, Running Bird sat quietly, trying to figure out why the planets zoomed in and out, depending upon which eye he used to view them.

For two minutes straight, he'd shut one eye, and then the other, murmuring, "Stars come close... stars go away... stars come close... stars go away."

Then Shaman Brave Wolf turned to him. "Running Bird," he said in a deep, echoey voice.

"—stars go away. Yeah?"

"You go dance now."

"Where? Over there with Rising Water and his friends?"

Brave Wolf nodded.

Grabbing his decorated club, Running Bird headed over to the fire and joined them, stomping and shuffling about, just like everyone else.

Hearing the chants being sung in their native Navajo tongue, Running Bird participated in that aspect of the ceremony as well (despite never having been taught the ancient language).

Then the chief called to him. "Running Bird! Come, Running Bird! It's time! The spirits are ready!"

Meeting him in front of the fire, Shaman Rising Water unsheathed a knife. He looked into Running Bird's eyes. "Hold out hand."

Running Bird reached out his hand, palm-side down.

Grasping it firmly, the chief turned it over, right-side up. And with the precision of a skilled surgeon, he cut each of their arms, just deep enough to break the skin.

Then he sang the sacred sorcerous verbiage needed to complete the transfiguration, and smashed their forearms together. And the campfire erupted like a volcano, illuminating the skies for miles around.

50

"I think you're full of crap!" Running Bird laughed, jumping out of the phaeton.

"Nuh-uh! I not full of crap!" The chief huffed, trying to maintain a straight face. "It was four years ago, and I remember it good because it was only a few months later when I had my vision, telling me to go save you from dying in desert."

"Uh-huh. And how big was it again?"

The chief looked down at his hands. And then he held them up again, separating them even farther apart than what they were either of the first two times he told the story. "I telling you, the fish I caught that day was *this* big! And it took me over one— no, *two* hours to reel him in! He a big fish! Really big fish."

"Oh really? And just what kind of fish was it?"

"What kind?"

"Yeah. You know. Was it a bass, or a trout, or what?"

"Oh. It was a... uhh... A 'monster fish!'"

"A monster fish?"! Running Bird whirled around toward him.

"Yeah, that's right." Rising Water nodded.

"There's no such thing as a 'monster fish!'"

"Is too! It was so big, I had to fold him in half to make him fit in the ice chest. And then he *still* barely fit!"

"Fold him in half?"! Running Bird exclaimed, peering down at their cool. "That ice chest is thirty-six inches long! Needing to squish him in there like you're describing would mean your phantom fish was over six feet long!"

"Yeah, that's right."

Running Bird laughed. "I'll untether Thunder and Lightning from the phaeton, and give them fresh water. You can go on in the hogan, and I'll be in, in a minute."

"Big. Big fish... *Monster* fish, it was." The chief continued babbling on his way inside.

Five minutes passed.

Ten minutes passed.

Twenty minutes passed, and Running Bird still had not returned.

Finally, Chief Rising Water went outside to go look for him. As soon as he exited the hogan, he noticed something peculiar: Lightning wasn't inside the wickiup.

"Running Bird! What taking so long? And why Lightning not inside, where it shady?"

He listened for a reply but heard nothing. "Now what that boy up to?" he muttered, walking over to the wickiup, where he found Running Bird standing in Lightning's stall. "What you doing?"

"Lightning came in here, got all jumpy, and then backed out real quick, like something scared her. I blew it off at first, but then when I tried to get her to come back in, she wouldn't. In fact, she won't come any closer than that." He pointed to where she was standing, about forty feet away. "What do you think her problem is?"

"Not sure. Did you look under her bedding?"

"Yeah. No rodents ran out when I kicked the straw around, and I couldn't find anything sharp on that ground that she may have stepped on. It doesn't make sense."

"When she came in, did she get a drink before she ran back out?"

"I think so," he replied, hopping up on the feed bin.

The chief made his way over to Lightning's water supply.

"I already checked that," Running Bird said.

Opting to inspect it himself, Rising Water placed his face just above her water and breathed in. "It smell fine." He lifted a cupped handful of it to his lips, slurping as he sucked some in his mouth.

"Eww, gross!" Running Bird made a face and turned away.

"Tastes all right too."

"Lovely..."

"Did you look inside what you sitting on?"

"Yup."

"What about all the stuff next to you?"

"Yeah. There wasn't anything in any of it that would have spooked her." He re-examined some of the nearby items in the chief's presence. "See? The spare saddle is clean, and the extra bridles in this tub are— OWWW!!" Running Bird fell from the feed bin, his body crashing to the ground. For he'd just been bitten by a rattlesnake that had been camouflaged by all of the looping leather reins inside the tub.

Launching itself with an insane amount of force, the reptile had slammed its jaws into his arm, drove its fangs deep into his flesh, and injected more than twice the lethal dose of venom into his bloodstream.

Surprised by the unforeseen turn of events, Chief Rising Water strolled over to where Running Bird lay writhing in pain. He contemplated what to do, but nothing really came to mind. So he looked down at his ailing pupil and asked, "Does it hurt?"

"DOES IT HURT?"! Running Bird screamed. "YEAH, IT HURTS!"

"Humph." The chief pursed his lips to the side. "Okay. Take arm out of sleeve, and hold it over here." The chief squatted down. "Let me see."

Grimacing, Running Bird unbuttoned his cuff and pulled up his sleeve, exposing his arm.

Rising Water looked at the bite mark; it was already engulfed by a grotesque bruise. He examined it for a moment. Then, with the most serious look he could muster, he looked Running Bird dead in the eye and said, "That *sucks.*"

Running Bird's jaw dropped open in disbelief. "Wha-ha-ha-hut?"! His voice quivered in the midst of his exclamation. "That sucks? What the hell kind of response is that? I'm about to breathe my last breath, and all you can say is, 'that sucks'? What's wrong with you? Do something!"

"Okay." The chief stood up, turned around, and started to walk away.

"Wait! What are you doing?"!

"You told me, 'Do something.' It's lunchtime. I hungry. So I go fix lunch now."

"Lunch? But what about *me*?"!

"What about you? I'll fix lunch for you too."

"Fix *me* lunch? Does that mean I'm not going to die?"

"No, you no die. You fine."

"I'm fine? But wasn't that a diamondback that bit me?"

"Yeah, that's right."

"But, they're deadly. So how am I fine?" he asked, making his way to his feet.

"Because you a shaman. Shamans can safely handle snakes and scorpions. You could drink their poison and still be fine. Now come on. Get up. I hungry."

51

"What's that thing that you're putting on?" Running Bird asked.

"It called a bolo tie," the chief replied.

Running Bird gazed at the lavish necktie, admiring the turquoise centerpiece. "It sure is fancy. I don't remember ever seeing it before."

"That's because I never wear it before."

"Really? Why not?"

"Liawatha gave it to me long time ago. Was a present. Very special present."

"That's nice. Why are you wearing it today?"

The chief didn't reply. He wasn't being rude; he was just in his own little world. "...yes, very special present indeed," he continued murmuring.

Throughout the entire morning, he scurried about in a most peculiar way—without saying a word—until he finally came to a standstill right in front of Running Bird. "Well, you ready?"! he asked, wearing a huge smile.

Running Bird looked at the old man like he had three heads. "Ready for *what?*"

"We go to river now."

"We go to— But why?"

"Better question is, 'why not?' I go out and tether horses to phaeton. You put on teguas. We go now."

After he departed, Running Bird stared out the door, into the distance. "Now what's gotten into him?" He brooded over his mentor's abnormal behavior.

The ride to the river was a quiet one. The chief continued smiling, and Running Bird continued wondering why.

Rising Water even closed his eyes from time to time, relishing every passing moment for nothing more than its mere existence.

Arriving at the river, they dismounted the horses and walked out into the water as usual.

What *was* unusual, however, was the horseplay that ensued. For it wasn't long until the chief called to Running Bird, and when he turned around, he splashed him in the face.

"Hey!" Running Bird hollered, shocked by the elderly man's adolescent outburst. "You goofball!"

"I not goofball!" He giggled, splashing him a second time before hopping to the far side of the river.

Running Bird gave chase. But when he started splashing him back, Rising Water began yelling "Truce-truce!" in the midst of his hearty laughter.

"Oh sure!" Running Bird laughed. "First you soak me, and then you call a truce, before I have a chance to get even."

"Yeah, that's right!" The chief embraced him. "I love you, son. I go lie down now. Time to journey to other side." Rising Water rested his hand upon the young man's cheek, and then sauntered away.

Watching him trek across the river, Running Bird tried to make sense of Rising Water's aberrant behavior, but it just didn't stand to reason. Snapping out of his stupor, he replied, "I love you too!"

Hearing Running Bird from the shallows, the chief threw his hand in the air, and proceeded up the riverbank.

His destination was simply that of a large, flat, waist-high boulder; yet it had an immeasurable amount of sentimental value to him. For it was upon its surface that he and Liawatha lay many moons ago, gazing up at the stars, when he asked her to become his wife.

As he neared it, a thick celestial energy filled the air—an energy so dense that it elevated his body atop the rock.

Seeing his mentor levitate rendered Running Bird speechless.

Rising Water carefully positioned himself in the center of the nostalgic stone, ensured his bolo tie was straight, pulled something out of his shirt pocket, and lay back.

Then, very deliberately, he rested his hands upon his chest, interlocked his fingers, and closed his eyes.

"He— he sure is— Wait! He called me 'son!' And told me he *loved* me! Did he say that it was time for him to journey to the other side, so he could lie down? Or if he was going to go lie down, because it was time for him to journey to 'the other side.'

"Oh my God! CHIEF!" Running Bird cried out, trying to leap through the water, flogging it with his arms in a futile attempt to sprint through the thigh-high river.

Just then, the cloudless skies unleashed a deafening, triadic crack of thunder, the gravel visibly jouncing in its wake.

Tromping wildly out of the water, Running Bird raced up the riverbank, fearing the unthinkable.

Upon reaching Rising Water, he fell at the base of the boulder on which he lay, in a state of utter exhaustion. "Chief?" he groaned, clawing at the stone slab, straining to make it to his feet. Tears streamed down his face. "I know I said I'd be happy for you. I just nuh-nuh-need a minute. And then I'll stop crying, I promise."

In the midst of composing himself, he noticed something in the chief's hand. It was the item he had removed from his shirt pocket just a moment ago.

Running Bird looked to see what it was. And despite his excruciating emotional pain, he did something that he didn't think he'd do again for the rest of his life: he smiled. For projecting from between Chief Rising Water's fingers was one of his most cherished possessions: the picture of him and Liawatha on their wedding day.

52

Back at the hogan, despite his gut-wrenching grief, Running Bird knew he must summon the strength to dig a grave for Rising Water. Under the scorching noonday sun, the arduous task nearly proved to be more than he could handle.

Countless times, he forced the steel shovel into the sandy soil, the ensuing scraping sound wreaking havoc on his eardrums.

Dime-sized blisters soon formed between his thumb and index finger, where the shovel's wooden handle had rubbed his skin raw; and salty, stinging sweat was streaming into his eyes.

When he finished, he picked the biggest, most beautiful sand verbena he could find, and laid it atop the grave.

Then he selected two leftover handles from the crafting of their decorated clubs, broke the "Y" ends off, and tied them together in the shape of a cross. Lumbering back over to the gravesite, Running Bird used the backside of his shovel to tap the cross into the ground.

Then, to conclude the ceremony, he got down on his knees, interlocked his fingers, and said a prayer.

At first, he was just saying what he had to say in his head. But then he began whispering.

And before long, his incoherent mumbling had evolved into a full-blown eulogy: "...and I'll always remember the great times we had, and everything you taught me. You once told me that a person's skin and hair are nothing. You compared them to the siding and roof of a home. I understand what you mean, and I believe you. I know you still exist, Chief; you just moved on to a different home—one where I can't see or touch you right now. But one day I will. And then I'll finally get to meet your wife, and you can say, 'Liawatha, this is my good friend, Running Bird. He the one who walk through river like drunken buffalo!'" Running Bird felt a tiny chuckle spring from his heart, and sneak its way out through his sadness. "Oh, Chief, I miss you so much. You just have no idea. If I had just one wish, I wish I could see you right now. You and Liawatha. I bet the two of you are so happy, laughing and running around like little kids! That would mean more to me than—"

"SCREEEL!!" Chills shot up Running Bird's spine. He whirled around, his eyes locking on Liawatha's favorite perch. "Oh my God!" His eyes bulged from their sockets. For atop the hoodoo—for the first time ever—he saw not one but *two* eagles. "Chief! Chief! Is that really you?"!

"SCREEEL!" the larger of the two birds replied.

Every single hair on Running Bird's body stood up.

Then both of the regal creatures spread their wings and took flight, playfully swooping and soaring together.

Running Bird tracked their every move. "This is amazing! They're so beauti— Ooomph!" He tripped over the exact same rock he tripped over when he saw Liawatha for the first time. And just like that time, he once again struck his head plenty hard on the boulder next to it. Although he remained conscious, he was rendered very woozy.

Pushing himself up to his hands and knees, he felt his ear to see if it was bleeding. It wasn't. "Damn, Barry's baseball bat's got nothing on that boulder," he mumbled, pulling himself to his feet.

Running Bird watched the two eagles for a little while longer, and then he headed back toward the hogan. But after taking only a few steps, he stopped dead in his tracks. "Barry?" he repeated in an airy voice. "Who— Wait a minute!" His eyes lit up. "Barry! Yeah! I remember!" he yelled, running around the hogan, thrusting his fists in the air. "And I— I am Dwayne Rader! Yeah, that's right! I *am* Dwayne Rader!"

Slowing to a walk, he pretended to approach an invisible acquaintance. "Well, hello there." He placed his forearm across his midsection and bowed at the waist. "I am very pleased to meet you. *My* name is Dwayne Rader. What's that? You don't remember me? Well, that's okay. Because, do you know what? I DO! I finally remember me! And I can tell you all about me! My mom's name is Julie. And I have a girlfriend named Jackie! And her parents are Clark and Joleen Ramsey. And—" Suddenly, every detail of his life rushed to the forefront of his brain. His eyes burst wide open, and chills surged through every fiber of his being. "Jackie!" Dwayne shouted, sprinting into the hogan. "Don't worry, baby! I'm coming!"

Racing around, he realized he had to slow down and think.

Mumbling his thoughts aloud, he devised a strategy: "Pack some absolute essentials, take the phaeton to town, tell Miss Mary what happened, and sell the horses to get enough money to pay for a ride to the closest bus station, and a ticket to go home. Good! Yes, very good plan!"

Dwayne grabbed an old suitcase from the wickiup, packed a few necessities, and headed toward the phaeton.

Before he reached it though, the larger of the two eagles swooped down and landed on the rock he'd just tripped over. "Eh! What are you doing down here?"

The humongous bird hopped down onto the ground; it began kicking sand in all directions.

"What are you trying to tell me?" Dwayne thought for a moment. "Oh, I know! You told me to dig there if I was still here when you joined Liawatha!" He rushed over to the rock, fell to his knees, and began sweeping the sand away.

In no time, he uncovered some boards. Feeling for the edge, he grasped one of them and pushed it off to the side.

Tingling with anticipation, Dwayne shoved his face in the crack to see what was in the hole. "Mason jars?"

To be certain, he removed two more boards and looked again. "Yup. Lots and lots of Mason jars."

He squatted down, reached inside the pit, and extracted one.

Wiping off the outside, Dwayne looked through the glass. "Oh, my!" he gasped, falling back onto his butt, his whole body shaking. "Is that what I think it is?" He unscrewed the lid and pulled out what was inside. "It is! It's money!"

Sitting motionless, he gaped at the cash.

Then he snatched up two more jars.

Peeping through a clean spots in the glass, he confirmed that they, too, were filled with money.

He looked up at the hoodoo. Both eagles were perched there, sitting side by side. Dwayne had not a clue what to say. Finally, he uttered four words. "Thank you. But how?"

And then it hit him. He *knew* how.

For the past three or four decades—maybe more—the chief had been panning for gold and cashing it in a little at a time. And it had added up over the years.

Dwayne peered back down into the pit. All of the jars were lined up in rows. There were ten rows, and each row contained twelve to fourteen jars. His eyes widened. "There's over a hundred jars in here!" He pulled the contents out of one of them. "And these are all one hundred dollar bills!" He counted them to see how many he was holding. The higher the figure rose, the faster his heart raced. "98... 99... 100. Okay, so if each jar contains a hundred bills. And each bill's worth a hundred... times a hundred jars. Let's see, that's a 'one' with four... five... *six* zero's after it. Oh my God!" He nearly fainted. "There's over a million dollars here!"

Dwayne's eyes darted skyward, his body trembling worse than before. "Thank you, Chief!"

"SCREEEL!" he replied, flying away with Liawatha by his side.

A few minutes later, in the midst of packing his suitcase, Dwayne noticed that one of the jars did not contain cash. Rather it contained a small envelope.

He dumped it out onto his palm. It contained three rings. All of them were gorgeous, but one must have been extra special to the chief, for it sported the largest, most perfect diamond he'd ever seen.

Forcing himself to calm down, he secured the jewelry in its own compartment inside his suitcase, finished packing the cash, and headed to town.

53

Approaching the livestock shop, Dwayne saw Kevin, Miss Mary's nephew, going up the stairs of her store. "Kevin!" he hollered, pulling back on the horses' reins. "Can you ask Miss Mary to come outside, please?"

"I'm sorry, Running Bird. But she has off today."

"Oh, no! Do you know where I can find her?"

"No. Is everything okay?"

"It's a long story. Do you know of anyone around here who has a car? I need a lift."

"I got a car, but I have a date in a little bit. If it wasn't for that, I'd give you a ride. Where do you need to go?"

"I don't know. I mean, the bus station. Or a train station, or something! I don't care! I'm heading back east."

"The bus station? I don't know of any buses or trains anywhere around here. The closest thing we have is an airport, and that's fifty miles away. I hate to tell you, but you're going to have a hard time finding someone to—"

"I'll pay you five hundred dollars, to take me there right now!"

"I'll go get my car. Stay put. I'll be right back."

"No, pick me up around back. Is John inside?"

"Yeah."

"Good. I'm going in to talk to him real quick. Then I'll meet you behind the store. Okay?"

"Okay."

Three minutes later, Kevin pulled around back. Dwayne gave John a hug goodbye, hustled down the steps, and jumped in the car.

No sooner did they pull away than Dwayne began smirking.

"What's up with you?" Kevin asked.

"It's just been a crazy morning. John was wondering why I had Thunder and Lighting with me, because he thought I was you, until we got to talking."

"Me?" He laughed, leaning up to look at himself in the rearview mirror. "Humph, I never realized it before, but we really *do* look like each other, don't we? Your hair's a few inches longer, and your skin's tanner than mine, but yeah, our facial features are a lot alike."

"Tanner? Do you think so?"

"Running Bird, over the years, your skin has somehow gotten darker than what some genuine Navajo's ever get. And look at how long your hair has gotten! Indian life has most definitely agreed with you, that's for sure."

Dwayne smiled. "Why, thank you, Kevin."

"Eh, no problem. So, did you and John get everything squared away?"

"Yeah, I told him to give the horses to Miss Mary when he sees her, and to tell her I said goodbye. I know how much he liked the chief's phaeton, so I gave *that* to him. He was—"

"Hold on! Why are you giving all of Rising Water's stuff away?"!

Dwayne turned to Kevin, wearing a very solemn look.

"Oh, no!" he gasped. "You mean?"

"Yeah." Dwayne nodded.

"When?"

"Earlier today."

"Are you okay?"

"I will be."

The two young men laughed, cried, and reminisced the rest of the way to the airport. Pulling into a parking spot, Kevin looked at Dwayne and smiled. "I sure am going to miss you, Running Bird."

"I'm going to miss you too," he replied, pulling the money he owed him out of his suitcase. "Here you are. Five hundred dollars, as promised."

"Excellent. It's a pleasure doing business with you. Have a safe flight, and make sure you keep track of all your stuff. It gets pretty crazy in there."

"What do you mean?"

"It's not laid back like you're used to. People rush around inside that place like their pants are on fire. My uncle lost his wallet in there once, and they wouldn't let him on his flight."

"Why not?"

"Because it had his driver's license in it. They won't let you fly anywhere, if you don't have some kind of ID."

"ID? I don't have a driver's license or any kind of ID! Now what do I do?"! He began to panic. But then his face lit up.

"What's going through that head of yours?" Kevin asked. "And better yet, why are you smiling at me like that?"

Like a shot, Running Bird dove back into his suitcase and pulled out another five hundred dollars. "Here you go!" he said, handing it to him.

"What's that for?" he asked, gawking at it.

"It's for you—just as soon as you sell me your license."

"Just as soon as I what? Oh, hell no! Are you serious?"!

"Yes. It's the only way I'll be able to buy a plane ticket to fly home. C'mon, even John mistook me for you, today. Just tell the DMV you lost yours. Wadda ya say?"

Squirming in his seat, Kevin deliberated on the offer for a moment. "Grrr... Oh, okay! Getting a replacement license from the DMV is going to be a pain in the ass, but for an extra five hundred bucks, I guess it's worth it."

"Aw, thanks, Kevin! You're awesome!"

"Yeah, I hear ya. Okay, here you go, Mr. Richardson." Kevin snickered, handing Dwayne his license.

"Who?"

"Mr. Richardson."

"Who's Mr. Richardson?"

"You are, you ding-a-ling! You're Kevin Richardson now!"

"Oh, yeah!" Dwayne laughed, jumping out of the car, grabbing his suitcase. "Goodbye, Kevin."

"Bye, Running Bird. Have a safe flight."

54

L anding at the BWI Airport, Dwayne exited the plane, retrieved his suitcase from the baggage claim, and hailed a cab.

Before long, he arrived at the Ramsey's. "That's odd," he said, looking at their residence.

"What is?" the cabdriver asked.

"There aren't any cars in the driveway. They should have gotten home from work hours ago. Do me a favor, and don't leave yet. I want to make sure someone's home before you take off."

"No problem."

Dwayne ran up the sidewalk and knocked on the door. There was no answer. He pounded on the door with his fist. But still, no one showed up.

Hustling over to the bushes in front of the living room's bay window, he cupped his hands, held them by his eyes, and pressed his face against the glass. All the lights were off.

Just then, an older lady emerged from the neighbor's house. "Young man! Young man! Just what is it that you're doing?"

"I'm looking for Jackie, but no one seems to be home. The Ramsey's do still live here, don't they?"

"Yes, but they won't be home for another hour or two, after visiting hours are over."

"Visiting hours? Where are they? The zoo?"

"My heavens, no! They're at the hospital again."

"The hospital? What's wrong? Who's sick?"!

"No offense, sonny, but we're a close-knit little community, here; and we don't go-ah spewing everybody's business 'round town, especially to strangers."

"But Mrs. Halperstam! I'm not a stranger! I'm Dwayne Rader, Jackie's boyfriend! Don't you remember me?"

"Dwayne Rader?" she murmured, tapping her chin. "Oh, yeah. I remember a 'Dwayne.' Real nice boy, he was. He's dead though. Died years ago, he did."

"Dead? Mrs. Halperstam, he's not dead! I'm Dwayne! Me!" Dwayne pounded his chest with both hands.

The short stocky woman waddled over to him in her muumuu, slurping the grease from her fried chicken dinner off her fingers along the way.

Leaning in close, she squinted, studied him for few seconds, and then backed away.

Unable to reach a solid conclusion, she fumbled about her bust in search of her glasses, which dangled from her latest flea market find—an ugly blue necklace composed of little hollow plastic balls.

Once she located them, she put them on her face and stood up on her tippy-toes. With her nose now merely inches from his, she leaned left, paused, and then leaned right.

Then she lowered her heels back down to the ground and announced her verdict: "Nope, you just ain't him!" She whirled around and headed home.

"Dammit!" Dwayne yelled, jumping back in the cab, slamming the door shut. "To the hospital! And hurry!"

55

"Whoa, boy!" the cabbie scolded Dwayne for jumping out of the vehicle, before he came to a complete stop. "Are you all right?"

"Yeah." He yanked his suitcase out of the backseat. "What do I owe you?"

"$79.50"

"Here's a hundred. Keep the change." Dwayne jogged up to the main entrance of the hospital with his luggage, entered through the automatic doors, and hurried to the information desk.

"May I help you, sir?" the hospital volunteer asked.

"Ramsey— Jackie Ramsey. What room is—" Dwayne was too winded to speak.

"Are you all right, sir?"

"Yes ma'am." He took a moment to breathe. "Can you please tell me what room Jackie Ramsey is in?"

"Let me see." She pecked away at her computer keyboard. "Ah, here we are. She's in room 122. Write your name in the guest book, clip this visitor's pass on your shirt, and then go straight down thatta way until you come to a pair of doors. Make a right.

Take the second hallway on your left, and 122 will be just ahead on your left— I mean, right. If you get lost, just ask any of the staff along the way, and they'll assist you."

"Thank you very much."

Dwayne skedaddled down the hall as fast as he could go, trying not to exceed a fast walk.

Reaching the first pair of doors, he broke to the right, paused at the first perpendicular hallway he came to, and tried to remember the directions he was given.

Proceeding to the second hallway, he glanced left, but at the last second, turned right… and plowed headlong into a priest. "Oomph! Oh, my! Father, I am so sorry!" Dwayne apologized, steadying the man. "Are you okay? Here, let me help you straighten your glasses." Very gently, he lowered them from his forehead to his nose. Then he placed the side support behind his ear, where it was located prior to their collision. "There we go. How's that?"

"Good as new. The last time someone used that much care situating my spectacles for me, I wasn't tall enough to be able to see over ma's kitchen table. Where are you off to in such a hurry, my son?"

"I'm looking for room 122. Do you know where it is?"

"Sure. Right down there on your right." He pointed in the direction he almost went, before he changed his mind.

"Ok. Great. Thank you, um..."

"Pastor Kimmel."

"Thank you, Pastor Kimmel."

Hurrying down the hall, Dwayne located room 122. He turned the handle and burst through the doorway.

Jackie and her parents gawked at the long-haired, dark-skinned, oddly attired stranger.

"Jackie?" Dwayne's voice crackled.

"Yes? Do I know you?"

"Jackie, it's me," he whispered.

Jackie's eyes widened and her jaw dropped open. "Dwayne? Dwayne, is that really you?"! she gasped, covering her mouth.

He tried to say "yes," but no sound came out of his mouth. So he resorted to nodding. *That*, she understood.

"Oh my God, Dwayne!" Jackie sprinted across the room and flew into his arms.

After much crying, a lot of embracing, and a few kisses, they began simultaneously asking questions and talking over each other, trying to untangle a four year mystery in mere seconds.

"Honey-honey-honey!" Jackie got his attention. "Let's start at the beginning. You go first. What happened to you? No one could find you. The rehab people said you just vanished one day."

"I remember starting the program," Dwayne replied, "but I somehow got left behind in the desert. I would have died, but this Indian rescued me.

"An Indian?"!

"Yes. A Navajo shaman named Chief Rising Water."

"But why didn't you ever call or write to us, to let us know you were alive? We thought you died, Dwayne!"

"I had amnesia, Jackie. For the last four years, I had no idea who I was, or where 'home' was—until just this morning.

"Is that why you're so tan? And why your pants have all those fringes? Because you've been living in the desert... with Indians?"

"Yeah, that's right. Now it's my turn. *Who* is sick?"

Jackie burst into tears.

So Dwayne turned to her parents for an answer. He locked eyes with Clark.

Without saying a word, Clark stepped to the side so Dwayne could see the little boy lying in the bed behind him.

Dwayne studied the child for a moment. Then he looked over at Jackie's parents. "Who's that?"

Clark swallowed hard, his eyes drifting to Jackie.

Dwayne's followed suit. "Who's that in the bed, Jackie?"

Clearing her throat, the young lady dug deep for strength. "That's Colby," she replied ever so softly.

"Colby?"

"Yes, Dwayne... he's your *son*."

Chills surged up Dwayne's spine and cascaded down his arms. "My— my son?" he gasped, peering down at the helpless child.

Jackie walked up to Dwayne. She reached out and held his hand. "Yes, Dwayne. We have a little boy together."

Dwayne wept with joy. He grabbed ahold of Jackie and embraced her. "I can't believe it. I— I just can't believe it! You're a mother!"

"Yeah." She giggled, wiping a tear from his cheek. "And you're a father."

"Hey, yeah!" Dwayne's eyes widened. "But wait! What's wrong with him? Why is he here in the hospital?"

Jackie took a deep breath. "I don't know how to tell you this other than to just come straight out with it."

"Straight out with what? What's wrong?"

"He's really sick, Dwayne."

"Sick? How sick? What's he have?"

"He has a form of brain cancer. It's—"

"Brain cancer? Okay, so let's get him some radiation treatment, to put it into remission!"

"It's not that simple. The cancer is rooted in a part of his brain called the corpus callosum. It's preventing the two hemispheres of his cerebrum from communicating with each other."

Dwayne looked down at Colby, and then back up at Jackie. "So, what does all this mean? How do we make him get better?"

Tears streamed from the young mother's exhausted eyes. "We can't. He won't. It's irreversible. His heart's stopped beating twice already this week. There's nothing anyone can do."

Dwayne looked back down at his son. "Oh yes there is," he mumbled.

"I'm sorry, honey," Jackie said, leaning in closer to him. "I couldn't hear you. What'd you say?"

Dwayne reached down and ran his fingers through Colby's hair. "I said, 'Oh yes there is.'" He repeated himself, his eyes remaining locked on his son's face.

"Huh? What do you mean?"

"Nothing. You stay here. I need to speak to your father, alone, out in the hallway."

Dwayne walked over to the door, opened it, and looked at Mr. Ramsey. "Sir? Please."

Clark exited the room with Dwayne.

Less than two minutes later, they returned.

Upon their reentry, Mr. Ramsey looked at Joleen and smiled; Mrs. Ramsey furrowed her brow in confusion.

Dwayne walked over to his suitcase, reached inside, and pulled out the envelope containing the jewelry.

Then he dumped the three rings out onto his palm, he pulled out two, and walked over to Jackie's mother with them. "Mrs. Ramsey," he said, giving her a kiss on the cheek. "Please hold out your hand." She did as he requested, and he put two of them in her hand. "I give you these rings as a gift. They carry with them an enormous amount of sentimental value, I assure you. Please cherish them always."

"Oh Dwayne, they're breathtaking! Yes! Yes, I will. Thank you."

Then, moving to his right, he stood before Jackie. "I know it's old-fashioned, but I wanted to ask your father's permission and get his blessing, before doing what I'm about to do." Dwayne cleared his throat, got down on one knee, and presented her with the most beautiful diamond ring that she'd ever seen.

Jackie's heart rate skyrocketed.

"Jackie, from the moment our eyes first met at that pretzel place in the mall—when you had that cute little bit of flour on your nose—I immediately fell in love with you. I knew right away that you were my soulmate. Jackie Ramsey, in front of your family, God, and our son, I am asking if you would please do me the honor of becoming my wife."

"Yes!" She wept and embraced him like never before.

Just then, a red light began blinking and an alarm sounded from one of the many machines Colby was hooked up to.

Two doctors stormed in, petrifying everyone.

But just as they began preparing critical emergency procedures, the alarm ceased.

"Miss Ramsey," the one doctor said, looking into Jackie's eyes. "You and your family need to say anything you want to say to Colby very soon; his time is drawing near, ma'am. I'm so very sorry."

Then both of the doctors departed, leaving the room of emotionally drained adults to their own devices.

"I have to hurry, honey!" Dwayne broke the unnerving silence. "There's not much time! Now listen carefully! In that suitcase is plenty of money for you to give yourself and our son a very good life, for a very long time. Use it however—"

"Money?"!

"Yes. I inherited it."

"Okay, but you're scaring me, Dwayne! Why did you say it was for *me* to give Colby a good life? Why didn't you say—"

"Hello, in there. May I come in?" a man asked, opening the door. "Ah, we meet again!"

"Pastor Kimmel!" Dwayne said.

"You two know each other?" Jackie asked.

"No. Well, sort of. We ran into each other out in the hallway when I was trying to find your room."

"Yes, I'd say 'running into each other' is an appropriate description." The jovial priest smiled. "When you asked where room 122 was, I didn't put it together at the time that you were talking about Colby's room. How's the young lad doing?"

"Not well," Jackie replied. "His alarm just went off again. And the doctors told us to say any final words that we want to say to him. They said—" Jackie bit her lower lip. "They said 'his time is near.'" She broke out into tears.

"Be strong, my child. Is there anything I can do to help? Anything at all?"

"Hold on, Pastor Kimmel!" Dwayne said, whirling around to Jackie. "I know this may seem inappropriate right now, but you have to trust me on this. Please, don't ask me why. It will all make sense soon. But can we please get married right now?"

"What? Here, now?"!

"Yes."

Pastor Kimmel looked most surprised. "Do you mean to say you are Colby's father?"

"Yes, sir. I am."

The pastor smiled larger than life. "May I please shed some light on your concerns?"

"Certainly, Pastor." Jackie whimpered.

"You're fiancé's suggestion is by no means inappropriate, Miss Ramsey. In fact, I feel like it would be viewed favorably in the eyes of the Lord for the two of you to be joined in Holy Matrimony, prior to your son's meeting with God, in his kingdom. And I would be honored if you would allow me to perform a very quick ceremony."

"Jackie?" Dwayne looked at her.

"Then I would be honored to become Mrs. Dwayne Rader today," she replied, "and to fulfill the dream I have had since our eyes first met, as well, Dwayne."

"Really? You felt it too?"!

"I knew it right away." She kissed him.

"Very well then!" Pastor Kimmel said. "Do you, Jackie Ramsey, promise to love, honor, and cherish this man, to have and to hold, in sickness and in health, for as long as you both shall live?"

"I do." Jackie smiled.

"And do you, um... pssst! What's your name, son?"

"Dwayne Rader."

Acknowledging his response with a smile and a nod, Pastor Kimmel straightened his glasses, repositioned his grip on his Bible, and proceeded. "And do you, Dwayne Rader, promise to love, honor, and cherish this woman, to have and to hold, in sickness and in health, for as long as you both shall live?"

"I do."

"Then you may kiss the bride."

And he did—very sweetly.

Then Jackie heard someone else crying. Peering over at her parents, she saw that it was her mother.

"Shhh, Joleen." Clark attempted to quiet her down.

"You hush up! My daughter just got married, and I'm allowed to cry if it want to!" She playfully smacked his arm.

The joyous moment was short-lived, however. For an ear-piercing racket suddenly erupted in Colby's room again. But it wasn't just one alarm this time—it was all *three*.

"This is it! I can feel it!" Dwayne hollered, running around to the opposite side of his son's bed, so that he was standing with his back facing the window.

"Dwayne!" Jackie screamed. "What are you doing? What can you feel?"!

"Jackie, I love you, honey, with all my heart! Take care of our son!"

Chills shot up her spine. "What? What do you mean?"! She could hardly hear him over the deafening alarms.

Knowing he had not a second to spare, Dwayne took a deep breath and raised his arms out from his sides.

The higher they ascended, the quieter his world became.

Although Jackie and her family continued to shout and flail their arms, Dwayne began perceiving everything in extreme slow motion.

Soon, he heard nothing at all.

As he closed his eyes, the very last thing he saw was Jackie reaching out to him with both hands, bawling, screaming his name at the top of her lungs.

Grimacing from the emotional agony, Dwayne squeezed his eyes shut as tight as he could, thrust his hands forward with all his might, and slammed them together.

A dim light began to glow from between his palms, awing everyone to the extent that they became still.

As the orb of mystical luminescence intensified, Dwayne's hands shook to the point that his entire torso trembled.

Wind whipped through the trees with monumental ferocity, stripping limbs of their leaves. And successive flashes of lightning filled the sky.

The window behind Dwayne exploded, cracks shooting out in all directions; and countertops throughout the facility shook, sending delicate surgical instruments plummeting to the floor.

Then the shaman's eyes burst wide open, and he hurled his hands down onto his son's chest, launching the sphere into the boy's frail, cancer-ridden body.

Colby's eyes surged open, and his back arched high off the bed; and at the same time, the wall-mounted television blew, showering the entire room with flurries of sparks.

Dwayne's son's eyes remained open at the conclusion of the maelstrom. But Dwayne's did not.

As Colby's body eased back down onto the soft linens, his father's collapsed to the floor.

Then, all became quiet.

When the chief surgeon snapped out of his stupor, his eyes darted over to the head nurse. "Get that man into the E.R. stat!" he shouted. "And page Dr. Nichols and Dr. Wickheimer! Now! Go!"

Then, whirling around to Colby's machines, he held his hands above the control panel's countless buttons. Poised and ready to react with catlike reflexes, he barked his next command: "Vitals! Hurry! Give me the child's vitals!"

"B.P 122 over 78! Pulse 69!" a nurse yelled overtop of... absolutely nothing. For all of the alarms had become silent, and all of the lights had stopped flashing.

The surgeon leaned back from the control panel and lowered his hands. "122 over 78?"

"Yes, doctor. That's correct. And pulse, 69."

"But how? That's not possible."

And then, the miracle happened. "Mommy?" a little voice could be heard calling out from the middle of the bed.

Every single hair on Jackie's body stood up. Even her eyelashes tingled. "Colby!" she screamed, pushing her way through the room full of doctors and nurses, with the strength of a thousand bulls.

Upon reaching him, she could hardly believe what she saw. It had been five months, one week, and three days since his brain functioned well enough for him to be able to respond to any stimuli, nonetheless talk.

Tears of joy poured from Jackie's eyes. "Colby! Oh my God, you're awake!" She sobbed, gently resting her face on his tummy.

And then something even more amazing happened: she felt two tiny little arms reach around her neck and squeeze. It was the first hug that she'd received from him in over a year.

56

itting in the waiting room, Jackie repetitively slewed her
diamond ring around her finger, waiting on an update.

When she and her parents saw the door begin to
open, they sprung to their feet. "The doctor's coming!" she blurted
out. But it wasn't the doctor.

"How's everyone holding up?" Pastor Kimmel asked,
emerging from behind the door.

The family closed their eyes, groaned, and sat back down.
"Oh, it's you," Jackie murmured in a humdrum tone.

"I'm sorry to disappoint you. The doctors will hopefully
know something soon though."

"Oh, Pastor, that was so rude of me! I'm so sorry. I didn't
mean to sound—"

"Shh, my child." He smiled. "There's no need to apologize.
I can't imagine how worried you must be. We should know
something soon."

Just then, the door opened again. This time, it *was* the
doctor.

"Which one of you is Jacqueline?" he asked.

"I'm Jackie," she replied, feeling her heart pounding inside her chest.

"My name is Dr. Nichols. Your son has remained alert and awake for the past two hours. During that—"

"He has? Oh my God, that's wonderful!"

"Yes. And during that time, we completed an extensive series of tests, analyzed new blood samples, and monitored his brain activity—"

Jackie waited on him to continue, but he didn't. He just stood there. "YES? AND...?"! She blew up.

"And nothing is showing up."

"Nothing's showing up? What do you mean? Your computers aren't working?"

"No, our computers are working just fine. I mean, all the tests we just ran... they all came back negative."

"Negative? Negative, how?"

"Negative for cancer. It's like he never had it at all. It makes no sense."

Jackie's whole body shuddered. Tears streamed from her eyes.

Clark and Joleen embraced her.

Even Pastor Kimmel shed a few tears. "It's a miracle!" he declared, pointing to the heavens.

"So Colby is healthy?"! Clark asked in the midst of his sniffling and nervous laughter.

"*Completely* healthy!" Dr. Nichols reassured him.

"Oh, thank you so much, doctor!" Jackie smiled, wiping her face and giggling. "And how about Dwayne? How's he doing? Will we all get to ride home together, you know, as a family?"

Dr. Nichols stopped smiling. He knew he had to say something, but he couldn't bring himself to do so.

"Doctor?" Jackie's voice cracked, realizing something was very wrong. She studied him more closely—and then it set in. "NO! Oh, doctor, no! Please! You have to do something! Go back in there and try something else!" She began physically pushing him in the direction of the operating room's entrance.

"I'm very sorry, Mrs. Ramsey. There was just nothing we could do."

Collapsing into her chair, Jackie buried her face in her hands and bawled, trembling as if she was on the brink of having a nervous breakdown.

57

"Vrooom, vroom!" Colby said, pushing his toy car along, playing with Clark out on the front porch of their home. "Ha, ha! I'm winning, Grandpa! You can't catch me!"

"Uh-huh! I can too! My car has a cool turbo-boost button that I can push. Watch. 'Poooshh!'" Clark snickered, pushing his toy car up ahead of his grandson's. "Look, I passed you! Now *I* am winning!"

"Hey!" Colby's eyes got as big as saucers, seeing that he no longer held the lead. "Oh yeah? Well, not for long, because I got a turbo thingy in my car too! Watch *this*! Wah-poosh!" he exclaimed, zooming his car back up in front of his grandfather's, giggling like crazy.

"Holy mackerel! Yours is super-*duper* fast! I don't think I'm going to be able to catch you!"

"Nope, you not, Grandpa! Wook!" Colby pointed at the extra wide blade of grass that he'd put on the porch, to use as a finish line. "My car crossed the line first. That means I won! Wait here!" He hopped up from his seated position, ran to the screen door, and flung it open. "I wanna go tell Mommy and Grandma real quick!"

But just as he was about to hightail it inside, Clark called to him. "Hey, Colby!"

"What?"

"When you get done telling them about our car race, tell your mother that Grandpa wants an ice cream bar. Ask her to give you *two*—one for each of us."

"Aww, cool! Good idea!"

Dashing inside, Colby headed in the direction of his grandmother's voice.

"...was a very nice service, honey. Funerals can sometimes be—"

"Guess what, mommy!" Colby shouted, running into the kitchen.

"Oh, my! I thought you were outside playing with Grandpa."

"Yeah, that's what I came in to tell you about! We was racing race cars and Grandpa was winning so I pushed my booster button so I could go really super fast and I won!" the long-winded lad said all in one breath.

"You did?"! Jackie replied. "That's fantastic!"

"Uh-huh! It sure is! It's—" Colby made a yucky face and pinched his nose shut. "Eww! Grandma, your house stinks! What's that smell?"!

"It's incense." Joleen laughed. "People burn it to freshen the air. I just lit a stick out in the dining room. It's supposed to make everything smell nice."

"Well it ain't workin' very good!"

"Oh my, little one!" She laughed. "Can you please go tell Grandpa that dinner will be ready in thirty minutes?"

"Sure. And Grandpa said he wants an ice cream bar. And he said to send me out with two, because he said I want one too."

"Oh, no! I don't think so!"

"But Mom, Grandpa's right! I *do* want one!"

"I hear you, little man, but dinner is in a half hour. And if you eat ice cream now, you'll spoil your appetite. Here, you can take two of *these* out with you." Jackie opened the freezer door.

Curious as to what the acceptable alternative was going to be, Colby stood up on his tiptoes and raised his eyebrows, hoping to improve his view.

"Here you go." She handed him two frozen treats. "You guys can have popsicles. They won't ruin your appetite."

"All right. Thanks, mommy."

Scurrying back outside, Colby plopped down beside his grandfather on the porch and held out his hand.

"Is that ice cream?" Clark asked, tilting his head to the side, scrutinizing the unfamiliar wrapper in an attempt to determine what it was, before officially accepting it. "That doesn't look like ice cream to me."

"Take it, Grandpa! It's making my fingers all freezy!"

"I don't know about this," Clark mumbled, warily taking it out of the boy's hand. He tore open the wrapper. "Aw, man! They duped ya, boy! This ain't ice cream, it's one of those other things!"

"Yeah, it's a poppy-sickle. Mommy said we ain't allowed to have ice cream because she and Grandma are making dinner. Poppy-sickles are still good, Grandpa. They're just not all creamy like ice cream, that's all."

"This stinks!" Clark griped, biting into the icy disappointment.

Colby brought his popsicle to his nose and sniffed it. "Mine doesn't stink. Inside the house is stinky, but my poppy-sickle don't smell like anything."

Sitting side-by-side on the front porch, Colby's comment didn't register in Clark's mind until he took a second bite. "Whus wong wif da house?" he asked, his mouth full of ice. "Duth eh really stink in 'nare?"

"Yup. It sure does."

"Why? Grandma isn't burning dinner, is she?"!

"Nope. She's burning nonsense."

"She's burning what?"

"Nonsense. She said people burn it to make the air smell nice, but I think it must be broke or somethin'."

"Oh! You mean, 'incense!'"

"Yeah, that's right."

"Ugh! Yeah, I agree with you. I hate when she burns that crap. It makes the whole house smell like monkey-butt."

"Yup. Sure does." He strategically licked what was oozing down the side of his popsicle, before it dripped onto his pants.

"Look at you!" Clark laughed. "Your lips are turning green from the lime flavoring!"

Colby pursed his lips out and rolled his eyeballs downward. "I can't see them."

The youngster turned to examine his grandfather's lips. But they looked normal because he'd quit eating his. "What's wrong, Grandpa? Don't you like your poppy-sickle?"

"It's okay, I guess. It's just not what I was expecting."

"You should give it to him, then. He'll eat it." Colby nodded to a dog that was standing at the end of Clark's driveway, urinating on his flowers.

"Quit peeing on my wife's pansies, pooch!"

"His name's not 'Pooch.' It's 'Caesar,'" Colby said.

"I don't care what his name is! He better cut that out or I'm gonna—" Clark clammed up before the remainder of his ill-tempered thought spewed from his mouth.

"Or you're gonna what, Grandpa?"

"Nothing. Nevermind. Say, how do you know that dog's name, anyways?"

"He told me."

"Oh, really?" Clark laughed. "That's cute. And I guess he told you he'd like to eat my popsicle, too, huh?"

"Yeah, that's right."

Seeing how serious the boy was, Clark toned down his demeanor and probed further. "Colby, you're kidding, right? I mean, you really don't hear dogs talk to you, do you?"

"You know what, that's exactly what Mr. Raman said when I told *him* about it," Colby replied just as he reached the center of his frozen treat. "Hey! Look Grandpa! I'm down to the poppy-sickle's stick!"

"Yeah. Forget about the popsicle for a minute, Colby. What about Mr. Raman? Who's he?" Clark sat on the edge of the porch, his anxiety skyrocketing.

"He... He..." Colby said, licking his lips and smacking his mouth. Then he looked at Clark and smiled. "Gwam-pa, my wips are weal-wee cold!"

"Ahhh! Colby, concentrate! They're cold because you're eating ice. Now listen, son. *Who* is Mr. Raman?"

"My pwee-school teech-ah."

"Your preschool teacher?"

"Uh-huh."

"Have you told anyone else that you can hear animals talking to you?"

"No."

"Okay. Good. Let's discuss it a little more after dinner. It's probably nothing, but I think we should see what your mother has to say about it. Okay?"

"Okay."

"Hey, while we're on the subject though, have you ever heard any other animals talk to you? You know, besides the puppy dog?"

"Uh-huh. I heard *him*, too." Colby nodded in an indistinguishable direction.

Clark surveyed his front yard, but he didn't see any other animals. "Who 'him,' Colby? I don't see anything."

"Up there in the tree. See? Way up top."

Fearful of what he might come across, Clark's eyes slowly climbed the tree.

Leaning back as far as he could, just before he saw it, he heard it: "SCRREEEL!!"

"Jeee-sus!" Clark cried out, his appendages flying every which way. "What was *that*?"!

Colby, on the other hand, remained still. "You're silly, Grandpa." He emitted a little giggle. "Do that funny dance thing again."

Clutching his chest and breathing heavily, Clark asked his next question in a much softer tone of voice. "What's that in the top of Grandpa's tree, Colby?"

"It's an eagle. Ain't he cool?"

"Colby, I've lived here for over forty years, and I've *never* seen an eagle within a hundred miles of here. What's he doing up there?"

Wiping the popsicle juice on his chin off with his sleeve, Colby looked up at him. Then he looked back at Clark. "He's sitt'n."

"He's sitting?"

"Yup. It looks like he's just sitting there, to me."

"And... and he talks to you?"

"Sometimes."

"May I ask what he says?"

"Different stuff. You know, like how much he loves me and Mommy. I've only seen him up there a couple times, not all the time."

Clark stood motionless, continuing to gaze upward in sheer amazement.

"Hey, Grandpa?"

Mesmerized by the enormous creature, Clark didn't hear him.

"Hey, Grandpa!" Colby tugged on his shirttail. "Who's Mr. Shipley?"

"Uh, your preschool teacher?" Clark murmured, still gawking at the eagle.

"No, that's Mr. Raman! I asked who Mr. Shipley is."

"I dunno. Some guy I guess."

"See, that doesn't make sense."

"What doesn't?"

"Well, one time, the eagle told me to tell you he said, 'Thank you for Mr. Shipley,' but you don't know him." Colby turned his attention back to the eagle. "I wonder where his home is."

Still contemplating the child's question, Clark said the name aloud several more times, deeming it more familiar each time he repeated it. "Mr. Shipley... Mr. Shipley... I *do* know that name, but from *where*? Mr. Ship—" He all of a sudden recalled hiring Mr. Ralph Shipley to represent Dwayne in court when he was arrested.

Clark's eyes widened, and chills shot up his back with the force of a freight train.

Gasping for air and feeling faint, he tried to compose himself in front of his grandson.

"Are you okay, Grandpa?" Colby asked, jumping to his feet, leaning in extra close to his face. "You're lookin' sorta green. You know... wike my wips." He pursed them outward to ensure his grandfather could see them.

"Yeah, Colby. Grandpa's okay."

"Then why didn't you answer me?"

"I'm sorry. What was your question again?"

"I said, 'Where do you think the eagle's home is?'"

"Well, Colby," Clark replied, "if I were a betting man, I would say, 'He IS home.'"

END

Acknowledgments

First and foremost, I want to thank God, and give Him all the glory for this remarkable achievement. I also want to thank my parents, John and Donna, for their unconditional love and support over the years. Thank you for never giving up on me. And hat's off to Deborah Perdue at Illumination Graphics for my awesome cover, Joni Wilson for all of her formatting expertise; and Ian Franzen, owner of College Web Pro, for my incredible website. And last but not least, my pre-readers, Marjorie Zent, Heidi-Finn Lombardi, and Anne Talbot; I could not have accomplished this without you. God bless all of you.

A Note from the Author

I just wanted to take a moment and sincerely thank you for reading my debut novel, *Teachings of a Shaman*.

And now that you've finished it, I have a small favor to ask of you: the next time you find yourself online, **please take a moment and log onto Goodreads.com, and rate my book** – or better yet – maybe even write a short review. ☺ I LOVE reading reviews!

I hope you loved it and rate it 5 STARS, but if you don't, I understand; I am a novice author who's very open to criticism, and I know I have much to learn. Rest assured I will be taking each and every comment to heart. Thanks in advance!

—Corey Stultz

Upcoming Releases

Before getting sober, Stultz spent twenty-one months in jail for driving while intoxicated. It was during this time—from behind bars—that he wrote not one but seven novels. As a prisoner, Stultz did not have access to metal utensils, nonetheless computers, so he scribed each book *in longhand*, using four-inch rubber pens and over 2,700 sheets of paper he obtained from the jail's commissary.

Stultz's works are listed below in the order he wrote them. His remaining six novels will be released as they become available. In the meantime, please visit **coreystultz.com** for updates.

A Simple Man (crime/detective)

Shattered Psyche (horror)

Private Malpractice (suspense/thriller)

Biological Control (sci-fi)

Teachings of a Shaman (fantasy/coming-of-age)

A Thousand Alibis (mystery)

Tormented (paranormal)

Made in the USA
Middletown, DE
13 July 2018